SOJOURNER TRUTH

Voice for Freedom

illustrated by Lenny Wooden

SOJOURNER TRUTH

Voice for Freedom

by Kathleen Kudlinski

ALADDIN PAPERBACKS

New York   London   Toronto   Sydney   Singapore

First Aladdin Paperbacks edition January 2003

ALADDIN PAPERBACKS
An imprint of Simon & Schuster
Children's Publishing Division
1230 Avenue of the Americas
New York, NY 10020

Designed by Lisa Vega
The text of this book was set in Adobe Garamond.

Printed in the United States of America
2 4 6 8 10 9 7 5 3 1

Library of Congress Control Number 2002107414
ISBN 0-689-85274-6

ILLUSTRATIONS

CONTENTS

SOJOURNER TRUTH

Voice for Freedom

Home in the Cellar

"Will it ever stop raining?" Belle shivered in her thin cotton shift. She stood next to her brother as he watched guests arrive at Master Hardenbergh's inn in Rifton, New York. The white people stepping out of the carriages were wrapped in cloaks and furs against the chilly fall air. Most of them didn't bother to notice the slave children standing at the corner of the porch. A few greeted them in Dutch, *"Goedenavond."* Belle ducked her head, not daring to answer. One woman called, "Good evening," then turned to her husband. "Why, aren't they just the cutest little things?"

"You know how I feel about slaves," the man

said. "Why, it's 1806! Slavery should be outlawed, even out in the country like this."

"Hush, dear," the woman scolded. "We're guests here." And they went in through the door.

Peter pulled on Belle's hand. "What did they say?"

"I reckon 'good evening' is English talk for '*goeden avond.*'" Belle drew a circle in the cold mud with her toe, then added, "I cain't guess what all the rest of those words meant. That lady sounds squeally as a piglet, doan' she? " Peter giggled and Belle let herself smile.

Master Hardenbergh's angry face appeared at the open top half of the door. "Get to bed!" he snarled. The slaves scampered back around the corner but stayed close enough to peek at the strangers. No one else came, so the children walked around to the back of the house. Belle cupped her hands to catch some of the water dripping off the eaves. "Maybe it will be sunny tomorrow," she said softly. "I could get dry and warm."

"Winter comes before warm," Peter said.

The two slave children stood in the shelter of the eaves, gazing out through the rain in silence.

Beyond the yard and a tidy stone wall, Black Creek swirled wide at the base of their hill. Past the empty fields stretching into the twilight, misty hills rose over a ragged tree line. In the distance Catskill Mountains loomed darkly. Somewhere out there the Hudson River flowed, deep and dangerous. Belle shivered again.

"We share a blanket tonight," Belle told her brother. In the window over their heads light flickered from inside the room. There was a lantern lit in there, a fire, and hot food. Belle could hear the laughter of Master Hardenbergh's guests and the clink of glasses. She stood on tiptoe in the mud and reached up to press her hands against the crack under the window. It felt warm against her fingertips.

"Puddle!" Startled by Peter's voice, Belle stepped back. Her bare foot sank ankle deep into cold water. She stared. By the light from the window she saw a puddle lapping at the cellar step.

"We've got to stop it!" Together the children pushed the mud into dams and dug channels, trying to keep the icy water from running down toward their beds.

Hands shoved the window open. "Belle! Peter!" Master Hardenbergh said. "It's getting cold in here. Close the shutters. Be quick or you get a licking!" The window slammed shut and the curtains were drawn. Belle and Peter reached up to unhook the heavy wooden shutters and swing them closed. Belle had to stretch to her full height to turn the latch that held the shutters. They moved to the next window, and the next.

"Children?" A tired voice called up from the darkness.

"Yes, Mau Mau," Belle answered promptly.

"Come inside."

Peter and Belle shuttered the last window, then padded down the stairs. Between them a thin trickle of water found its way over the sill and dripped downward. "Quiet now," Mau Mau said from the far corner of the floor. Only eight, Belle was slender, graceful, and so tall she had to duck her head under the timbers of the ceiling above. Faint lantern light shone through the cracks in the floor of the inn. Even on the darkest night Belle's feet knew the path back to her family's sleeping space in the corner of the cellar. To either side a dozen slaves lay snoring or whispering together in their places under ragged blankets. Mau Mau and Baumfree were talking quietly in the darkness.

"Is there a cover for us?" Belle whispered.

There was no answer. Belle and Peter began pushing damp straw into a pile on the floorboards near their parents. Their mother tossed a tattered quilt their way as the children settled down on the bedding. "Thank you, Mau Mau." Belle sighed. Soft murmurs and a steady dripping sound filled the cellar around them. Belle leaned against Peter's bony back and shivered again. He rolled away and pulled the cover off her shoulder. "Hey!" Belle yelped in surprise. "That ain't fair!"

A sudden thump of hobnail boot on the timbers overhead made everyone go silent.

"Well, it ain't fair, Mau Mau," Belle grumbled.

Mau Mau hissed. She reached out in the darkness and slapped her daughter. "You hush your voice!" Belle froze in embarrassment, but her mother wasn't done. "You mind the story of the Master and the baby?" she asked.

Belle nodded and squeezed her eyes shut. She'd heard the story often enough that it came to her in nightmares, but now Mau Mau told her again. In a whisper barely louder than the rain outside, she began, "One morning a slave mama could not make her baby stop crying. The Master sighed. He looked mean at the little black baby. He scolded and he slapped the mama, but she could not make that baby be quiet. So you know what the Master did?" Belle held her breath. Peter's back had gone stiff.

"Well, now," Mau Mau went on as if she were telling the story to herself. "The Master took that baby by the feet. He swung him, *bam!* into the wall. Then he handed the body back to the mother. And that baby never did make another sound. Now you both go on to sleep."

Belle tried to make her body go limp on the straw. A crack in the boards beneath her shoulder pinched her skin, but she didn't dare complain. She shifted her weight, and the mud beneath the board made a sucking sound. Sleep? How could she sleep after that story? She couldn't get the picture of that baby out of her mind. *Why did Mau*

Mau have to tell that story again? The only worse one was about Belle's sister being stuffed into a box and sold one winter day. Ten brothers and sisters gone—all of them sold before she was born. Mau Mau just kept telling their stories over and over. Plus the one about the crying baby. Belle's eyes filled with tears, but she didn't dare cry. That made her nose run. She sniffed, then had to sniff again.

Her father's bed boards creaked. "Let's say the Jesus prayer now," he murmured.

Mau Mau took a deep breath and the four of them whispered together, "Our Father, who art in heaven . . ." Belle wondered briefly who that Jesus person was, but it didn't matter. The chant of familiar words calmed her mind. Her body relaxed at last.

"Amen," they finished the prayer together, and Belle slipped into sleep.

"Move!" Belle waved her arms at the sheep the next afternoon. The flock climbed the steep hill toward the barn. "Shoo!" The ram turned and glared, his horns gleaming in the slanting rays of the sun. Belle hurried to the far side of the flock across rocks and damp leaves. "Woof!" she barked, and clapped her hands to spook them. She bent down, pretending to pick up a rock. The nearest sheep broke into a trot and the others followed. The whole flock clattered up the stony hillside rushing for the safety of the barn.

Other slaves were milking the cows and pulling down hay. One of them swung the gate shut behind the panicked sheep. "What did you do to them?" he asked, grinning.

Belle shook her head. "I jus' know what to say to them," she teased, and scampered back down the hill. Peter had the chickens gathered in for the night too. He was waiting at the foot of the hill.

Together they ran out to help their father in the field. They wandered up and down rows of dead corn stalks, digging rocks out of the soil. They carried the ones they could lift to the edge of the field. A wall was forming there, made all of dug-out rocks. When they found a rock too deep to dig out themselves, Peter called out "Baumfree!"

Belle watched her father hurry over with a big stick to pry the rock out. It was no wonder where he'd gotten a name that meant "tree." He was the Hardenberghs' tallest slave. Baumfree's hands were long and thin like Belle's; his legs and arms were built long too. Belle looked at her father's back, bent beneath years of labor. His hair was gray as ashes. "Peter and I can tote that rock," she told him. "We are strong as mules."

"My first wife was like you," Baumfree told her. "Young and strong—and stubborn, too. Always pushing me aside to help, leastways until she got sold away."

Belle leaned close. "Was your second wife like me too?"

"Only had her a little time afore she was sold. Don't rightly remember her." Baumfree wiped his forehead, then glanced up at the house before going on. "Now, your mau mau, Betsey, she never slacked once, through all those babies. And before the ol' Master died and give us to Master Charles, why, we had us a cottage and a little garden. Oh, and weren't we s'posed to keep it too." Baumfree was standing straighter Belle noticed. "Your mau mau and I, we . . ."

"What are you telling them about me?"

"Mau Mau!" Belle dropped the rock she was carrying. She wanted to hug her mother, but one look at her face made Belle step back. Mau Mau had been crying again.

"Go and play," Belle's mother said, her voice dead tired.

Peter and Belle stared at each other. Play? But there was still a little light in the sky. Surely there was more work to do! "Shoo," Baumfree said.

They ran to the creek bank. Belle pushed her way through the dried cattails to a space she'd cleared back in the summer. Wind whispered through the reeds standing stiff on the far bank. Clouds gathered over the mountains. A fish jumped—*kersplash*—right in front of them. The two slaves sat on the smooth moss trying to guess where the fish would jump next. It felt strange to sit still. "What's that?" Bell stood up and pointed.

"An otter," Peter was on his feet too. They watched it dive and tried to hold their breath

10

until it came up again. The otter surfaced nearby with a fish wiggling in its whiskery mouth. In the last of the sunset light, the fish's scales gleamed gray-silver, its gaping mouth was bloody red. The otter tossed it up and caught it again with a flash of sharp white teeth and a *ka-runch* that carried over the water. In an instant, the fish was gone and the otter dove again. Belle swallowed hard.

"Why, here they are." Mau Mau's voice surprised Belle. "They made a place to rest your old bones, Baumfree."

As her parents pushed through the reeds into their hideaway, Belle pointed at the moss. "There's space for you too Mau Mau."

But the slave woman stood stiff and tall, staring over the horizon. Belle followed her gaze. The first evening star was just beginning to glimmer. Belle's breath caught. It was time for the star story. She looked back at Mau Mau. Tears—silent tears—were running down her mother's face again. "Look at the stars, Belle," Mau Mau said. "My ten other babies are somewhere, gone, all sold away from me. But they all are looking at

the same stars tonight." She sighed. "God willing."

Belle looked down at Peter and tried to imagine her ten older brothers and sisters. Where were they? What did they look like? How old were they? Would she ever meet them? She stared at the star so hard that tears gathered in her eyes too.

"Now, you mind what I say, Belle," Mau Mau said. "You too, Peter. When you are sold, no matter where they take you, no matter how they beat you, you look up at the stars whenever you can." Mau Mau's voice broke for a moment. "I'll be looking up too."

Belle put her hand on her mother's arm, but Mau Mau just shook her away. Loneliness swept over Belle.

"God lives up there," Mau Mau said, "in the sky. When you are beaten or fall into trouble, you must ask help of Him."

"What will He do, Mau Mau?" Peter asked.

"He will always hear and help you."

Belle wrapped her arms around her body and hugged herself tight. "Can you tell us all their stories tonight, Mau Mau?" she asked. "The others."

13

"We have a whole winter to tell tales," Mau Mau said.

"You don't know that neither, Betsey," Baumfree said. He groaned, struggling to his feet. "We will light a pine knot tonight and listen till it burns away in the cellar."

Belle and Peter raced up the hill, eager to get their table scraps and gather around the torch. Once the stories started, they never seemed to end. When Mau Mau and Baumfree were done telling of the loss of each child, the other slaves told their tales of pain and hope. But that night, long before the knot sputtered out, Belle sneaked away. She tiptoed up the steps to sit alone under a sky full of stars.

Poor Sheep

"What will you give me for this slave girl?" The auctioneer glared at the crowd. "Come now, fellows, she may be only nine or ten, but you can see she is going to be a big, strong worker." He pinched the muscle on Belle's arm.

Next he bellowed a whole string of strange words. *English,* Belle guessed. She stared at him. *He knows both ways of talking!*

"Built like a scarecrow," one of the farmers said in Dutch. Somebody else said an English thing and most of the farmers laughed.

Belle squinted in the summer sun as she scanned

the fields. Mau Mau and Baumfree were too old to work now. No one would buy a worthless slave, so they had both been set free after Master Hardenbergh died. But where were they now?

Suddenly the auctioneer pushed her to walk in a circle. He barked more English at her. When Belle didn't move fast enough, he pulled her top lip up for the crowd to see.

A tall stranger said something loud. He was looking right at her. Belle didn't know what to do. Then the man pointed at the Hardenbergh's sheep huddled in a pen nearby.

The auctioneer thumped Belle on the back, said something more in English, and held up her arm. Then he looked at the stranger. So did Belle.

The stranger shook his head no, pointed at the sheep and grumbled loudly. Belle wondered desperately what they were saying. They were talking about her. Was she being sold to this man? Or were the sheep?

The auctioneer said something angry sounding. The stranger raised his hand.

"Sold!" the auctioneer yelled. Now he was speaking in Dutch again. "For one hundred dollars to John Neely, trader from Kingston—assorted livestock." While someone wrote things down in a book, Belle was shoved toward the stranger.

"Come on," the man said.

Belle stared at him. *Come?* That English word sounded like the Dutch word *komen*. She knew what that meant, and she decided to take a step toward the stranger. Before she could move, the auctioneer shoved her so hard she fell to the ground in front of the tall stranger.

He hooted and said something as she scrambled to her feet. "John Neely," he said, pointing at himself. "Master Neely."

"Master." That sounded like the Dutch word *meester*. "Master Neely," she repeated carefully.

He nodded and pointed at her. "Your name?" he asked.

"Name" sounded a little like *naam*. "Isabella," she said, pointing at herself. "Belle." The stranger began talking again. Belle could tell he was asking a question, but she didn't know how to answer. He pointed toward the sheep and gave her a gentle

17

push. He pretended to herd the sheep along and pointed to her.

"*Ja,*" she said, and nodded. She knew what to do. "Shoo!" she yelled at the sheep. They ambled down the road at her familiar call. "Woof!" she barked at them. That made the man laugh, and he got up on his horse. "Come!" he called to her. *Komen,* she thought, and followed, driving the sheep before her.

"Good!" he called to her. It sounded like *goed.* Belle relaxed. She was doing something right. She herded the sheep for miles through the New York countryside. For the first few hours Belle tried to remember the dirt roads so she could find her way back home. She *had* to say good-bye to Mau Mau and Baumfree. Soon she was lost and the sheep were stumbling with exhaustion. "Poor sheep," Belle said, trying not to cry.

At last the man turned off the road. The sheep staggered after him. Belle just stared. The stone house was little and trim, and beyond it the Rondout Creek flowed deep and wide. A dock jutted into the creek. Barrels and baskets lined the dock. Back at the house a round woman stepped out of the doorway. Belle guessed it was Master Neely's wife. She shrieked something ugly. Belle did not need to know what her words meant. The Mistress was clearly surprised—and angry.

"Come here," the woman yelled at Belle. Belle walked forward. Mistress Hardenbergh had never invited her to come into her home. This white lady seemed very nice. But when Belle stepped over the wide stone doorstep, Mistress Neely slapped her hard.

Belle staggered back out. "Wash first," the woman said, and glared at her. Belle tried to figure out what she wanted. *Wazsh? Furst?* It didn't make any sense at all. The woman slapped her again. Belle turned and ran to hide behind Master Neely.

"Belle speaks no English," Master Neely said.

"Speak" sounds like "spreken," Belle thought. *He's right. I speak no English.* "Ya, Meesteres Neely. *Sprechen nee Engels.*"

Mistress Neely slapped her again and said very slowly and very loudly, "Belle *will* speak English."

❈ ❈ ❈ ❈

20

Belle did learn to speak English, slowly. After a few weeks at the Neelys she knew enough English to avoid being slapped all the time. She knew that "Get up" meant she should leave her bed on the floor. "Get firewood" meant she should gather sticks and logs for the hearth fire that kept the house blessedly warm. "Slop the pigs" meant taking the kitchen garbage out and throwing it into the hogs' wooden trough. And she couldn't make any mistakes in her own speech or she would be smacked again. Learning a new language was hard, but Belle Neely knew she had to do anything they wanted. She was their slave now.

One evening, when she had gone out for firewood, John Neely called to her from the barn. Belle danced across the snow moving her bare feet as fast as she could so they didn't freeze. Master Neely seemed to be in a hurry too. He was carrying a handful of long, stiff twigs as he pointed the way into the wooden barn.

As soon as Belle ducked into the barn's darkness, she felt the twigs slap against her back. "Why?" she tried to ask, but Master Neely hit her again. Over and over he raised the twigs and slashed at her shoulders, her back. Belle fell to her knees and Master kept whipping her. "Why?" she screamed, and "No!" and then, "Mau Mau!" and finally she just screamed in wordless pain. She held her hands up over her head to protect her face, and the blows fell on her arms instead. At last Master Neely stopped, panting. He staggered out of the barn.

Belle cowered in the straw trying not to weep aloud. If Master Neely heard her crying like a baby, he might come back and slam her head against the wall. She could feel blood trickling down her back. "Why, why, why?" She shook her head. Had she done something wrong? The pain made it hard to think. *No*, she decided. She hadn't done anything wrong. There was no reason for this. It made no sense.

When she could stand, Belle staggered to the water bucket. She pulled her torn shift off her back and rinsed the blood away, whimpering as she tried to make sense of this attack. Suddenly her breath caught in fear. Maybe a Master didn't need a reason to hit his slaves. That would mean there was no way to know when it might happen again. No way to avoid it. No place to run in this freezing winter weather. No way to protect herself against a grown man, either. She sobbed aloud in terror. It might happen again right now!

"Belle!" It was Mistress Neely calling. "Where is that firewood!"

Belle pulled the rags of her shift about her and stepped back toward the house, numb with fear. As she walked across the barnyard she felt silent tears streaming down her face. *Like Mau Mau,* she thought. Mau Mau had been beaten and survived. Belle had seen the scars. Other slaves had been beaten. They all knew this hopeless fear. That was just how it was to be a slave. Belle stopped and looked up at the stars. *Mau Mau!* She remembered that her mother would be looking up, and her brothers and sisters too. And that God lived up there in the sky. Shuddering with the cold, Belle repeated the Lord's Prayer until Mistress Neely called again.

❖ ❖ ❖ ❖

Belle lay stiff and aching in her warm corner of the floor that night, trying to think of all the ways she could please Master Neely. Maybe she could keep it from happening again. She said the Jesus Prayer and she began praying for Baumfree to come and rescue her.

After half a year her nightly prayers were answered. Baumfree limped into the farmyard and took his daughter into his arms. "What have they done to you?" he asked. The sound of the beautiful Dutch words in his dear voice made her begin crying, but silently. She had gotten good at that.

Baumfree went back and talked to friends who arranged for a new Master to buy his daughter from the Neelys. "Never was much good," John Neely said as she left.

Martinus Schryver was a different kind of Master. He ran a noisy, crowded tavern and fished in the nearby Hudson River. Belle, now almost eleven, carried the great slimy fish up from the river to the house. She worked outdoors in the tavern garden, planting, hoeing, and picking. Belle drank the beers that the Schryvers sold and learned to smoke a pipe from the men in the tavern. She hauled water from the well, fed the animals, and did some of the cooking, too. Mistress Schryver slapped Belle only when she forgot some of the day's tasks or when she didn't move fast enough. Master Schryver never beat her with sticks. It took months before the sick fear dulled—the fear of being beaten anytime, anyplace, and for any reason.

This new Master trusted her to run errands in nearby Kingston. She got used to dodging the carriages and stage coaches rattling down the cobblestone roads of the town. When there were no white people watching, Belle sometimes walked right on the dirt sidewalks, peeking through the windows into grand wooden homes. She strolled past the county courthouse with its great, high dome and stared at the churches, too.

God didn't live in the churches, she knew. He lived above the clouds, and she often talked to him when she was alone in the garden or in the fields beside the Black Creek. "Now, God," she'd say loudly to the sky, "If I was you an' you was me, and you wanted any help, I'd help ye." She would raise her voice even louder and scold, "Why don' you help me?"

When God seemed to do something to make her life easier, she always promised to be good in return. When she got second helpings of food or a few moments free from work, she might tell God she would stop saying the wickedly funny things that made people laugh. After a whole day when no one hit her, she might vow to stop swearing, even though the Schryvers did it all the time. She bargained with God too, staring up into the sky and telling Him what she would do if He helped her. She couldn't make herself keep all those promises, but it always felt good to talk to God.

One night the Schryvers held a grand ball. Belle scrubbed and baked, washed and swept and dusted until the tavern sparkled. She pulled the heavy chairs and tables to the sides of the great hall and carried in huge bowls of spiced cider and wine. When the guests arrived, Master Schryver let Belle peek at them through the kitchen door.

There was so much to see! The women were wearing fancy high-crowned white caps. Their long rustling dresses had so much starch pressed into them that they shone in the candlelight. When they twirled in the dance, their skirts flared, showing layer on layer of white hidden beneath, plus white cloth on their ankles, and tiny little shoes.

The men wore their Sunday best and everyone sang and drank and danced until late in the night. Then the men reached into little pockets in their vests and took out gold toys. These snapped open and the men would stare into them, then snap them closed again, complaining about the time. The fiddlers were still playing when Belle curled up in her corner of the kitchen floor to sleep.

At cock's crow the next morning she sneaked out onto the lawn and danced as if she were a fine lady. She sang the rowdy songs she had heard at the ball, remembering every word. As the first birds began chirping over the creek and the bank beyond, the great white sails of sloops glided up the Hudson River.

A shrill whistle cut through the dawn and Belle

ran out to the tip of the dock to look out at the river. A strange boat went by with no sails up at all. It didn't even have masts. On its sides huge paddles splashed water and great chimneys spewed black smoke and clouds of steam. Belle stared open-mouthed. Its whistle screeched again and it slowed, then seemed to stop still in the river's current. Slowly, grandly, the ship began to turn. Belle watched until it headed downriver toward New York City again.

"Belle!" Mistress Schryver yelled from the house. "Where's the water? There's no fire! You didn't start coffee water boiling!"

Belle sprinted up the lawn to the well and dipped up buckets full of water. She hooked one bucket to each side of the shoulder yoke and hurried back to the kitchen. She knew she deserved the smacking Mistress Schryver gave her for playing when she should have been hard at work. As Belle rushed back outdoors to fetch wood to feed the cook fire, she was still humming the tunes from the ball. If only she could belong to the Schryvers forever!

Surprising Friends

"You will call me Mistress Dumont," the short, round woman announced, "and this is my daughter, Gertrude." Belle glanced at the woman standing in the tidy kitchen. Gertrude stood beside her in a ruffled dress. Behind them two other white girls wiped their wet hands on stained aprons. Clearly these were not members of the Dumont family. They were paid helpers, Belle guessed, looking for only a moment before lowering her eyes. She could be hit for staring—if these new owners were the hitting kind.

"How old are you, Belle?" Gertrude asked.

Belle had no idea. How would anyone know such a thing? She stared at the floor trying to think how to answer.

"You *will* show my daughter respect!" Mistress Dumont said. "Tell her how old you are." The mistress reached out and grasped Belle's earlobe with her fingernails. Belle gasped with the pain. All on their own her hands rose to protect herself.

One of the servant girls laughed aloud.

"Kate," Gertrude scolded the girl, "laughing like that is mean. Mama," she went on, staring at Belle, "she looks just a little older than me. Maybe she's thirteen?"

Mistress Dumont let go of Belle's earlobe. "I'll have to watch you close, girl," she said. "I don't trust the looks of you."

"Yes, Missus," Belle said, her eyes filling with tears. She missed the Schryvers' warm bustling kitchen. When their tavern business stopped making money, they had to sell her. But did it have to be to this woman? Belle glanced at her new Mistress's stormy face and sighed.

Mistress Dumont made Belle's life miserable. She was never happy with what Belle did and often slapped or pinched her. She told Belle to do the hardest, dirtiest chores, the ones that the hired girls didn't want to do. The Mistress even made Belle sleep on the floor of her bedroom at night to keep her company.

Still, Belle liked Master Dumont from the very start. He was kinder than his wife. A Master had the right to beat his slaves—or even kill them—for any reason, or no reason at all. Belle knew that now. Yet John Dumont never hit her unless he believed she deserved it.

Kate, the kitchen girl, was different. She never missed a chance to tease or pinch or trip Belle. There wasn't anything Belle could do about it. Kate was white.

One morning while Belle was out milking the cow, Mistress Dumont called her back into the kitchen. "Who do you think will eat these?" Belle only had time to glance into the pot of potatoes boiling on the fire before Mistress Dumont's hand slapped against the back of her head. The water in the pot was filthy. Mistress Dumont hit her again. "You lazy girl!" she shrieked. "You didn't rinse them at all, did you?"

I did! Belle wanted to argue. But the water was dirty. Who would believe her? She looked around the kitchen at Mistress Dumont's angry face, at Gertrude's worried eyes, and last, at Kate's face. Kate was smiling.

"Sorry, Missus." Belle ducked her head and quickly grabbed a rag to protect her hands as she lifted the pot off the fire. "I'll do it over." Mistress Dumont got in one last smack as Belle staggered past with the pot. She tossed the potatoes into the pig trough, drew water from the well, rinsed the pot and refilled it. She peeled new potatoes and hauled in extra wood so the fire would bring them to a boil quickly.

The next morning Belle was milking the cows when Mistress Dumont screamed "Belle!" It had happened again. The potatoes Belle had gathered and carefully peeled were cooking in the pot over a fire Belle had started before the roosters crowed—and somehow the water had turned filthy.

This time Mistress Dumont's shrieks called the whole family into the kitchen. The girls gathered and stared and the three farm slaves stared in through the windows. "You see what I mean?" she screeched to her husband. "Belle might be a good worker for you, but she never does anything right for me!"

"Are you sure it was Belle?" the Master asked his wife.

"How dare you question me in my kitchen," Mistress Dumont said, her voice cold with anger.

Belle was bruised for days after that.

"Belle!" Cold shivers traveled up Belle's arms at the tone of Mistress Dumont's voice. It had been a week since the last beating. "You get in here. Now." Belle pushed the milking stool out of the way and grabbed the half-full pail of milk. There was no way to avoid the hurt she knew was coming now.

"Just look at those potatoes!" Mistress Dumont screamed as Belle slunk into the kitchen.

"Mama," Gertrude said quietly from the corner where she and Kate were standing.

"Not now," Mistress Dumont said. "I am fixing to teach this nigger slave a lesson once and for all."

Belle flinched. Mistress Dumont's words hurt as much as her hands sometimes.

"Mama!" Gertrude yelled.

Suddenly the kitchen was quiet. Everyone stared at Gertrude. "Mama, Belle didn't dirty that water," the girl said firmly. "Kate did."

"No," Mistress Dumont said. "I know this one." She poked her finger into Belle's chest so hard that Belle had to step back. "And she's"—poke—"no"— poke—"good." Belle could feel a bruise forming on her chest already.

"Mama," Gertrude insisted, "I hid behind the door and watched. After Belle went out to the barn, Kate scooped up some ashes from the hearth and dropped them into the water."

"She wouldn't do such a thing." Mistress Dumont stood tall and stared at her daughter. "Why, she is a white girl."

"I saw it, Mama," Gertrude said. "Here." She grabbed Kate's hand and held it out. It was smudged with soot.

Belle risked a look right up into Gertrude's blue eyes. *Why would she do such a thing,* she thought. *And for me?* Belle was flooded with thankfulness. She didn't have a chance to say it out loud, though.

34

Mistress Dumont had grabbed a broom and was chasing Kate around the kitchen and out into the yard. Pigs and slaves scattered out of their way. The geese hissed and honked. Chickens fluttered wildly and the dog barked. Belle watched for a moment and went back to make up a fresh pot of potatoes.

Gertrude wasn't the only friend Belle had at the Dumonts. The Master sometimes protected her from his wife's temper. He bragged about her to his friends, too. "She can do as much work as half a dozen white people, and do it well." He had even said that right in front of her.

That made Belle work all the harder to please him. She stayed awake at night thinking of ways to make him happy, and got up early to do extra work. The other slaves called her a "white man's nigger." They hated her for working extra hard just to get the Master's attention, but Belle didn't care. After all she had lived through, she felt lucky to have a Master like him, a warm dry floor to sleep on, food to eat, and clothes to wear.

❀ ❀ ❀ ❀

Sometimes the Dumont slaves left the farm. They would gather for Saturday night parties or Sunday meetings with slaves from other farms. There they would tell stories, talk about their Masters, share food, dance, and talk about God. News traveled on these occasions along with the slaves. Belle heard that her mother was well. Belle worried, knowing that her parents were getting old and Baumfree was very weak now. She sent messages back to her parents with slaves who lived near them. And she told their stories at the parties.

Saturday night dances were nothing compared to the Pinkster carnival. Pinkster was bigger than Christmas and New Year's Day put together. Every spring the slaves and free blacks in New York State gathered outside of Albany for a week-long celebration of black culture. Slaves who had been born in the United States learned about their ancestral homeland from blacks who had been kidnapped from Africa. One of the men was chosen to be "King Charles" of the carnival. A new king ruled every year in every city where Pinkster was held.

Carnival booths sold spicy foods, powerful

drinks, and strong tobacco. The endless sound of drums filled the air. Blacks wore special clothes and feathers and had their faces painted. At Pinkster they learned songs and dances from Africa, along with other traditions handed down through generations of slavery in America. Wind and string instruments played through wild party nights.

Whites called this holiday Pentecost. They said it celebrated the day when Jesus' friends were told to go off and preach about Him. All that the whites did was go to church. Belle didn't care about that kind of party. She loved the wild dancing and singing, the drinking and costumes of a carnival. It was a chance to meet new friends from many towns, to act wild, and to feel free.

Except for some Saturdays and Pinkster, the Dumonts kept their slaves close to home. Church was forbidden, as was listening to readings from the Bible. Belle still prayed loudly to God though, promising Him anything just so Master Dumont would keep on liking her. Sometimes it seemed that Master Dumont knew her thoughts just like

God did. Belle knew they both—the Master and God—could keep track of everything she did by writing it in their books. Even things she had forgotten were written down. Belle knew that writing and reading were for God and white people.

At the Pinkster celebration when Belle was sixteen, she danced with a handsome young slave named Robert. Belle was very tall and graceful, strong and lively. Robert was as dark as she, and even taller. His voice was getting deep and his rich laugh rang out at all of Belle's jokes. Robert made up a foolish bird dance to make her laugh too. They learned that their owners lived near each other, and Robert promised to visit her someday.

A few nights later, as Belle was shooing the chickens into their pen, she heard a hissing sound coming from the spring house. She glanced at the geese. All three were sleeping quietly, their heads nestled under their wings. Belle stared at the spring house. A black hand appeared out of the gloom of the door and waved a feather at her. Belle looked around first before waving back.

The hand motioned for her to come closer. Belle could not resist. "Robert, is that you?" she whispered. The hand turned like a goose's head to look at her, then lowered in a threat, goose style. Robert stepped out into the moonlight. "You lovely, silly goose!" Belle said, surprising herself. Silently Robert danced up to her, pretending to be a courting bird. Belle pretended to ruffle her feathers and then stretched her long neck out so he could nibble at it with his goosy hand.

Then they flew, flapping their "wings" across the pasture, free and wild in the moonlight. Finally they fell together onto a bed of ferns, laughing. Robert "flew" to the Dumonts often after that night. Over the weeks, Belle grew to love this wonderful, playful young man.

Robert's owner was George Catlin. When Master Catlin learned that Robert was sneaking visits with John Dumont's slave Belle, he was furious. What if Robert and Belle started a family? The Dumonts would own all of Belle's babies! George Catlin wanted Robert to marry one of his own slaves so he could keep their babies. He told the boy never to visit Belle again. But Robert was in love. He kept sneaking back to the Dumont's farm.

One afternoon George Catlin and one of Catlin's slaves followed him. Belle, sick that day, watched from an upstairs window as Master Catlin began beating her beloved Robert. It was horrible to see, and then it got worse. Robert was knocked nearly unconscious but still Master Catlin kept beating his body.

Belle began screaming, "Oh, God! God, help him! Master! Master!" The Dumonts ran to see what was happening.

"Stop, George!" Master Dumont yelled. Master Catlin kept kicking and hitting Robert. "Stop this instant!" John Dumont pulled George Catlin off. "There will be no slaves killed on my property."

"Very well," Master Catlin grumbled. He grabbed the dazed Robert and jerked him to his feet. Limp and bleeding, Robert was dragged away. Belle was left weeping.

Robert never came to visit her again. His will and his spirit were broken along with his heart. As soon

as Robert could walk again, George Catlin made him marry a girl slave on his property. Robert died a few years later of injuries from Catlin's beating.

Belle's mother had died suddenly too. Perhaps it was from something she caught in that cold, damp cellar at the Hardenbergh's. After Mau Mau was gone, there was no one who could care for Belle's father, Baumfree. He was far too old and weak to get food. No owner wanted a worthless slave. Belle had visited him when she could in his shack in the woods, but it was a ten-mile walk just to get to him. The Dumonts kept her working nearly every waking minute so there wasn't time to hike out to bring scraps of food or clothes to her own father. One winter Baumfree finally starved to death alone in his shed.

Belle cried silent tears now for so many: By the age of seventeen she had lost her brothers and sisters, her true love, and now her mother and father. She didn't bother to wonder if she would ever find happiness. Why should she hope? She was a slave.

Baby Slaves

"Belle," Master Dumont said one day, "you're getting old enough to make us some babies." Belle blinked and swallowed hard. The Master rested his hand on the cow she was milking and went on. "Thomas will be your husband."

Thomas? Belle kept her eyes down. *But Thomas is old!* She tried to remember what she knew of him. He'd been married before and had other children, now sold away. He worked hard. He had never given her any trouble. He had a strong back with only a few scars. But Thomas was short and bent, almost like Baumfree. His hands were dry and bony, his face was wrinkled, and his hair was gray. He was old.

Belle thought of Robert's warm smooth skin, his thick bushy hair, his wide, easy smile. Her eyes filled with tears. "But, Master . . . ," she whispered.

"Tomorrow."

"What?" she yelped.

"Don't you raise your voice with me!" Master Dumont warned.

"Yes, Master," Belle muttered, and went on milking.

"This will be a good match," Master Dumont mused aloud. "Thomas has been a hard worker since we got him back. And his babies always come big and fast and strong."

Something deep inside Belle wanted to weep and scream, to hit, to run. But that would make Master Dumont angry. He would beat her—and she'd have to marry Thomas anyway. She told herself that this had to happen sooner or later. She had always known it. A "marriage" like this had happened to her own mother. It happened to every slave. She took a deep, even breath and picked up the full bucket of milk.

"Looks like the day will be sunny, Master Dumont," she said, and left the barn.

* * *

That evening Belle looked down the hill toward the river. Thomas was walking up the road, driving the cows before him with a long twig. He was only tapping them lightly to keep them moving. Belle let herself smile just a bit and walked down the hill to meet them.

"You been told?" Thomas asked. Belle didn't bother answering. They walked side by side for a few steps. "I won't hurt you," he said, clucking softly to hurry the slowest cow along. Belle kept walking. "I do anything for you," he added, putting a hand on her shoulder.

Belle laughed quickly and moved away. "We are slaves. We are like bees with empty hives. We have no honey to give each other."

"When they sold my first wife away, I ran after her."

Belle didn't answer, but she was listening very closely. Thomas must have really cared for her to risk being killed as a runaway.

"I followed the slaver all the way to New York City."

"You did?" Belle tried to picture New York City. She couldn't.

"It's a big, big place, that city, Belle. There are more people and shops and carriages and houses there than there are feathers on a flock of geese. Noisier, too. I plumb couldn't find her. But Master sure found me. And he brought me back. And taught me good."

So that's where the scars come from, Belle thought. She stared at Thomas but he just kept walking toward the Dumont barn.

"They gave me another wife after a bit, then sold her off too. Said she wasn't worth the food she ate. I reckon it was 'cause she had no babies."

Belle stepped closer to Thomas when they walked the last steep stretch to the big red barn. Part of her hoped he would put his hand back on her shoulder. He didn't.

Belle was seventeen when her first child was born in a little cabin on the Dumont property. "Master says we can name her whatever name we want," Belle said, astonished. "Can we name her after my sister Diana?" Thomas nodded, picked up his shovel and went back to work on their own little garden plot. Saying "Diana" helped Belle keep her long lost sister's memory alive. It also helped Belle remember that the new little baby was not hers. Master Dumont owned the tiny slave and could sell it any time he wanted to.

"Diana!" Belle stood to stretch her back and leaned on the hoe to watch her daughter run across Master's field. Even at six the girl had begun to look like her mother, with dark black skin, long legs, and long graceful fingers. Belle smiled. She would be a good worker for the Dumonts.

Master had been angry when her next baby, Thomas, had sickened and died. "I was looking forward to that one," he said. "As big as you are, Belle, a son by you would be strong as a horse."

Belle listened to the new baby wailing from the basket hanging from a tree branch. "Well, Master, I've made you another son," she said aloud. That boy surely had good strong lungs. "I'm almost done with this row," Belle told

Diana. "Rock Peter back to sleep."

"But, Mama, Peter is hungry," Diana said. "Me too."

"You want a beating from me?" Belle threatened. "You rock the baby." Belle hated to be harsh, but it was important that slaves learn to obey quickly and without talking back. Besides, she could feed Peter when she got done with the row. Diana hurried to rock the baby. She sang as she pushed the basket back and forth.

"Belle! Come up here this instant!" Mistress Dumont's voice carried down into the field. "My baby needs milk." Belle sighed and straightened up again, then bent backward to stretch her body. Her breasts felt full. There would be enough milk for both Mistress Dumont's baby and her own.

"But . . . Peter is hungry!" Diana said.

"Hush your mouth!" Belle yelled back at her daughter. Then she turned and trudged up the hill.

Mistress Dumont was waiting at the door. "Where have you been?" she scolded. "My baby is near starving, and you are out playing in the field. . . ." Belle didn't wait to hear any more. She pushed into the kitchen and was unbuttoning her dress before she was halfway to the screaming baby lying in its goose-down cradle. She pulled her breast out with one hand and, with the other, threw lace covers off the little white baby and picked it up to feed.

"You watch how you hold my darling!" Mistress Dumont warned. As Belle nursed the hungry child, Mistress Dumont babbled on. "I swear, I don't know if it is wise to have you feeding my baby. Just look at your breasts." The servant girls turned to look. The kitchen slave looked. Master Dumont turned to look. The mistress wasn't done. "Your breasts are ugly. After all the children I've had, my body is still beautiful."

Belle fought against answering. Mistress Dumont looked fine because she had never fed her own children—that, and she wore a corset laced tight to keep her belly flat.

"Sally," Master Dumont said, "that is enough." Belle looked at her Master. If she said "thank you" out loud, the Mistress would start a screaming fight again. Belle could never say thank you enough to this wonderful Master. She looked down and shifted his baby to her other breast. When he was full and sleepy again, she settled him back into his fluffy bed and hurried out to Peter, screaming in his basket. There was almost enough milk left.

Over the next few years Belle and Thomas added another baby girl to their family. Every evening they crowded into the little cabin, where Belle told them stories her mother had told her, tales of loss and terror. They said the Lord's Prayer together, too.

One night they talked about the new law in New York State. "All slaves born before Independence Day 1799 are going to be free," Thomas explained to his children.

"Oh, when, Mama?" Diana asked.

"Your papa and I will be free as butterflies in 1827. That will be a few years." Belle took a deep breath and hugged her tiny new baby girl, Elizabeth. "But you children will not be set free yet. You girls still have to stay with Master Dumont until you are twenty-five, and Peter, you will have to stay until you turn twenty-eight." She hated this part of it.

"But you'll be working like a servant, not a slave," Thomas said.

"What's it like to be free, Mama?"

Belle thought about Mau Mau, sick and dying with no money for a doctor. She thought of her own father, dying with no owner to feed and care for him. It was too awful to talk about. "I don't know," she lied.

"Well," Thomas said, "I've seen plenty of free men. They don't have owners, so they don't get beatings. If you are free, you can go anywhere you want, anytime you want. You can get paid money for doing what we do for Master Dumont. I saw blacks in New York buying things in stores. For themselves. To keep." The children's eyes reflected wonder in the soft light of a burning pine knot. "Those free blacks were wearing shoes and fancy clothes and tall hats," Thomas went on, remembering. "You can do that when you are grown and free."

"I want to go now," Peter said. "I would buy toys and sugar candy in New York City. Why do we have to wait so long?"

"The Masters are in no hurry to let us go,"

Thomas told his son. "Can you just see Master Dumont milking his own cow?" The cabin filled with laughter at the thought.

"Or," Diana said, "Mistress Dumont slopping the pigs?"

Now everybody got into the game: "Or herding cows?" "Or cutting wool off the sheep?" "Or fetching water from the well?"

As the laughter died, Belle said quietly, "Laws can make white people obey even when they don't want to." She shook her head in awe, imagining the power.

"Master Dumont promised me he'll give us a cabin and land to live in when we're free," Thomas said. Belle was surprised he would say this, especially in front of the children. There wasn't much love in their marriage. There never had been. Belle knew she hadn't picked Thomas to marry and she wasn't sure she would pick him to be free with. "A home of our own," Thomas was saying. "It sounds good, but I don't know if we can trust Master Dumont."

"He told me he'd let me go a year early," Belle

told him. "If I work hard." She patted the children lying around them on the floor. "I do trust Master Dumont. I'll be free in the spring."

But when the springtime came, Master Dumont would not let Belle go free the way he had promised. "You hurt your hand, girl. Without that finger, you couldn't have given me a full year's hard work. I still own you, girl."

Belle stood silent before him, stunned by the hot anger filling her body. This wasn't fair. He'd promised. And she'd waited so long to be free. . . . She looked down at her fingers, twisted where the scars were thickest. One was shorter now, cut clean off.

"But I work as hard as any two slaves," she said, astonished at herself for speaking out. "You always said that." She braced herself for a beating, but none came. Belle began to breathe easier.

"How can I let you go now, Belle?" Master Dumont said. "There has to be a hundred pounds of wool in the barn that needs to be spun into yarn." Master Dumont held his hands out at his sides. "You are my best spinner."

Belle blinked. Master Dumont had never talked to her this way before. And he hadn't beaten her for speaking out in anger. *Besides,* she told herself, *he was right.* The wool needed to be spun.

She hated spinning, but she *was* good at it. He had even said so!

Her anger was gone somehow. "I suppose I can stay until the wool is spun." Belle felt confused inside.

"That would be fine." Master Dumont said. He pointed at her thick waist. "Besides, I'll give your next baby a good home here with me."

Belle's last child, who was called Sophie, was born before the wool was all spun. The Dumonts had sent five-year-old Peter to a neighbor, Dr. Gedney, to work. Thomas and Belle fought about her wish to leave. "You don't know how frightening it is to run," Thomas told her, "and how bad it is to be caught." Belle flinched, remembering the scars on his back.

"But it wasn't right to promise me I'd be free, then break that promise," Belle argued. Her anger grew all through the summer as she washed

Dumont's wool. She seethed as she combed out the tangles. The spinning wheel whirred as fast as she could make it spin and still twist the wool fibers smoothly. Piles of yarn grew along with her anger. Belle planted Dumont's fields. She hoed his weeds and harvested her Master's crops. It was all work she shouldn't have to do.

Now and then she told him so too. "You got no more call to ask that of me," she'd say, or "I'm s'posed to be the one just a'setting there now, Master. You should be a'toiling." Sometimes she would challenge him. "How do I know you be telling me the truth—this time?" But in the end she obeyed all his orders.

The extra summer of slavery gave her time to think—and to pray in a leafy hideaway down on the bank of the Hudson River. "I want to run away, God. I should be free now," she told the sky, "but Master Dumont needs me. He's been good to me. And I've done right by him. But the Master went back on his word. What do I do, God?"

By fall Belle had made up her mind. The answer came to her while she was praying. "Go!" It seemed that God had told her, Himself. Nothing in her life had ever felt so right. She would leave. Not run away, exactly. Just walk off.

And be free.

She, Belle, had decided something for herself. The thought flooded her with a whole new feeling. It wasn't quite fear, for God had told her to do this. It wasn't quite hope, for she was too afraid of what might happen. It was excitement, but there was more—something she could never have felt as a slave.

Standing up to Dumont made Belle feel proud.

It was a feeling Belle liked.

Give Me My Son!

"Belle? Belle Dumont?" Maria Van Wagenen stood openmouthed at her door. The white woman's bonnet quivered as she looked from Belle's face to Sophie, squalling in her arms. "Has your baby fallen ill?"

"No, ma'am." Belle stood tall, looking down on Mr. Van Wagenen's head as he hurried to the door. Belle took a deep breath. "I left Master Dumont's this morning before dawn. I am not going back."

She watched the Van Wagenens stare at each other for a long moment. Sheltering a runaway slave was against the law. Belle knew that. She

58

would only be a slave for another few months, but little Sophie belonged to Master Dumont.

"I stopped at Mr. Levi Rowe's first," Belle said. "He is on his deathbed, so he could not shelter me and baby Sophie."

"Oh, Issac!" Maria buried her face in her husband's chest. Her hands left floury smudges on his vest. "Poor old Levi!" she sobbed.

"He told you to walk all the way to us?" Issac Van Wagenen asked Belle. "That is ten miles! You must be tired. Come in and sit down." Maria wiped her eyes and hands on her broad apron, then opened the bottom half of the door.

Belle had to duck her head to enter their small cottage. "Mr. Levi said you were abolitionists too."

"That is true, Belle. We think slavery should be abolished. It should be against the law. It surely is against God's law."

"Then you will keep me until Master Dumont comes?"

The Van Wagenens looked at each other again while the baby cried. "John Dumont will come here?" Issac asked.

"Of course," Belle said. "But I will not go back with him." It sounded so good to say it aloud.

Issac was shaking his head, but Maria just clucked her tongue. "Now, Belle, you must feed that poor little baby while we wait. Issac will leave to give you privacy."

"Oh, there's no need to go," Belle began, but Maria stared at her husband until the man stepped out into the yard. Then Mrs. Van Wagenen turned away too, and began kneading biscuits on the table. Belle shook her head in surprise. What was secret about feeding a baby? Soon suckling sounds replaced angry squalling.

"You will be safe with us," Maria said toward the biscuits.

"Belle!" Master Dumont's voice roared through the open half of the door. "Belle, how dare you run away from me! Come out here!"

No, Belle thought, though she did not dare say it to his face. Instead she stared at her master silently. His face was angry and red. Though it was cool this afternoon, sweat dripped off his brow.

There would be a terrible beating if she went back, Belle knew. She didn't care.

"Hush, John," Mrs. Van Wagenen scolded. "You'll wake the baby."

"It's *my* baby!" Master Dumont thundered over the door. "If you don't come back with me now, Belle, you will go to jail!"

"I can do that," Belle said as calmly as she could, "but I won't go back with you."

"Wait!" Mr. Van Wagenen trotted across the lawn. "Wait! Nobody is going to jail!"

"Then my nigger comes home with me now."

"Not if we buy her from you," Maria Van Wagenen said from behind Belle.

"Ha!" John Dumont snorted. "You? You told me once that having slaves is a sin, remember?"

"We'll take Belle off your hands for twenty dollars," Issac Van Wagenen held up a fistful of bills.

Belle swallowed hard but didn't move. Master Dumont was looking right into her eyes—and Belle looked right back. She could hardly breathe with excitement.

"That noisy little pickaninny is mine too," he said, still staring.

"We'll take the baby off your hands for five dollars," Maria Van Wagenen said. "I reckon she wouldn't live without a mother's milk anyhow."

John Dumont said, "Ah, you keep them both." The Master shook his head. "Belle has grown too sharp-tongued to keep her around my other slaves. She is a troublemaker." He grabbed the cash from Issac's hand, turned on his heel, and stalked off down the road.

No one moved in the kitchen. Sophie slowly quieted, cooed, then went back to sleep. "Thank you, Master Van Wagenen," Belle said softly.

"I'm *not* your Master, Belle. You will work here as a servant. We will pay you for your labor, do you understand? You are not a slave."

"You and Sophie can sleep in the bedroom." Maria pointed to a ladder leading up to a loft.

"Belle?" Mr. Van Wagenen asked. "Would you help me in the barn this afternoon?"

Belle stood, silent, a smile pulling at the corners

of her mouth. She couldn't ever remember being asked to do something. She'd been ordered, commanded, and told what to do with every minute of her life, but never asked what she *would* do. Belle smiled broadly. "I'd be pleased to help you, Master Van Wagenen."

Isaac and Maria read the Bible in the evenings. Belle loved listening to the old, old stories. Some were as sad as Mau Mau's. Others were full of hope. She learned of the slaves in ancient Egypt and their long sojourn, wandering here and there in the desert, never stopping until they came to a land of milk and honey—and freedom. She heard all the stories Jesus told. She listened openmouthed to the story of Daniel. The good man was thrown into a den full of wild, hungry lions and then a rock was rolled over the door of the cave. When the rock was moved the next morning, there stood Daniel, not a scratch on him. "My God hath sent His angels and hath shut the lions' mouths," he explained. Belle loved the old-fashioned words, too, and learned them by heart.

The Van Wagenens were good people and kind to Belle. She fit in with them now. She had stopped drinking and swearing, habits she'd started long ago in the Schryvers' tavern. She tried to control her temper and to be "godly," not sinful. It was what she had heard from the Van Wagenens and their church friends. For months Belle lived the "holy" life, turning away from earthly temptations.

But when springtime came, her playful spirit bubbled up again. She began to think about Pinkster and the chance to go dancing and drinking with her old slave friends at the great carnival. She found herself humming the rowdy songs, remembering men like her dear Robert, and yearning for all that excitement again.

Part of her couldn't wait for the wild party. The other part was proud she had put all that behind her along with slavery. As she hoed and planted, washed and spun for the Van Wagenens, her mind fought between being holy and letting herself slide back into sin. "God!" she cried to the sky. "Help me." But the beat of Pinkster drums echoed in her head until she thought she would split in two.

"Mistress Van Wagenen," Belle said one day in June, "I do believe Master Dumont will come for me today."

"He can't take you." Maria chuckled. But she wasn't laughing as John Dumont pulled his wagon into the yard that afternoon.

"I'm going home with you," Belle announced. She had decided. She wanted the fun and the wild excitement of the Pinkster party, and she knew the Dumont slaves would be going.

"No, Belle," he said, smiling. "You had your chance to come back."

Undaunted, Belle rushed into the house to grab Sophie. When she came back out, Master Dumont was still there. Belle began to climb into the wagon and froze in horror.

What was she doing? Going back into the house of slavery? Where people were beaten and starved and shamed? And all for the sinful fun of drunken dancing?

And God knew.

He was watching. And God was strict and angry,

terrible in His power. And He saw everything. That's what she'd heard in the Bible.

Belle crumpled to the ground in fear. He would never forgive this. Nor, she thought, would He forgive all those promises she had made over the years. She wanted to apologize, to beg forgiveness, but she couldn't speak to one so huge. She crouched, weeping in the dirt while John Dumont drove off, shaking his head at her foolishness. She sobbed as little Sophie toddled over and patted her head. She screamed and trembled while Maria Van Wagenen took her little girl indoors. Belle knew her life was over.

When the emotional storm passed, she stood up, surprised. She was still alive! Belle felt a strange peacefulness. Someone had stood between her and God, protecting her; arguing for her life. "Who are you?" she whispered, though she already knew in her heart: Jesus, someone to protect her always. She stood tall, full of spirit. With Jesus on her side, Belle knew no one—not even God Himself—could harm her.

"Missus Maria," she gasped as she entered the

kitchen. "Jesus visited me! Me! I was just a slave, but He is my friend. He is yours, too!"

"Why, Belle, are you preaching to me?"

Belle laughed. "I am, ma'am. How can I talk about anything else?" Her voice was especially low and full of joy. "I love you." She stopped, startled by what she'd said. "I purely love everyone today. And I want them all to know what I just saw, sudden as a flash of lightning."

Maria Van Wagenen just laughed. "Preach all you want, Belle, but we need to get the breakfast dishes washed here."

Belle grinned and swung out the kitchen door, buckets in her hands. She was free. She was full of the spirit, and now she knew she had to share it with everyone.

At last the Fourth of July, 1827, came, and the New York State law finally freed Belle. The law said that her daughters had to stay and work for the Dumonts until they were twenty-five years old, and her sons until they were twenty-eight. Then they, too, would be free. On her freedom day, Belle went to her first church service. A Methodist preacher was leading worship in a house in Kingston. The owner of the home and his friends sat indoors in the shade while Belle stood outdoors with other blacks, watching the service through an open window. She swayed with the prayer. She wept as others "witnessed," telling how they had found their faith. As the minister called out the words, she sang along with the hymn.

Belle joined a church, thrilled by the spirit she found there. She heard more of the Bible read aloud. She loved the story of Lot's wife, turned to a pillar of solid salt because she paused to looked back, almost changing her mind after leaving a city of sin. Sitting with her friends in the pews kept for blacks at the back of the church, she sang hymns, witnessed, and prayed joyfully. In church she found rules to live by, and answers to all her questions about handling her new freedom.

"Your preaching is so wonderful, Belle," the Van Wagenens told her. "You should go out and tell the world."

Belle was ready to go traveling with her message of joy, but first she wanted to go home and make sure her children were safe.

Mistress Dumont had news for her when Belle went back one day to walk Diana, Elizabeth, and Sophie to church. "By the way," she said, "you may be interested. Your son, Peter, has been sold south. After we sold him to the Gedneys, they packed him off to Alabama."

"No!" Belle shrieked. Inside her chest, her heart had stopped. The South? Slaves in the Southern states were never set free! They died by the thousands, baked dry in hot fields. "My Peter is only six! What do they want with my baby? I'll never see him again!"

"Ugh," Sally Dumont scoffed. "A fine fuss to make about a little nigger."

Belle's breath caught. She couldn't believe Mistress's words. Worse still was the thought behind them. Belle drew herself up tall. It didn't matter that she had no money; God would help her get her son back. Belle felt as if she held the power of a nation inside her. "I'll have my child again."

Belle made her way to the Gedneys and stormed into Mrs. Gedney's kitchen. "Give me my baby Peter!" she said.

"*Your* baby?" Mrs. Gedney sounded angry. "What about *my* baby? My daughter, Eliza, married that Alabama planter, Fowler." She said the name like it was a curse word. "He's the one who bought your stupid little boy. My Eliza is a thousand miles away down in Alabama, poor thing."

Belle left in disgust. Eliza was a grown woman and white. She *chose* to marry a Southerner. Her own little Peter had been stolen, plain and simple. This wasn't unusual. Instead of setting their slaves free when the law demanded it, some New Yorkers sold their slaves off to Southerners. They made some money, but it was against the law. Gedney had broken this law. He had sold a slave out of state.

The law! That was the answer. It was the one thing that even whites like Gedney had to obey. But Belle had no idea how the law worked. She walked to a home nearby where Quakers lived. People of the Quaker faith had long fought against slavery. They would know what she should do.

"Oh, God," she prayed as she walked to a well-known Quaker's house, "make the people hear me. Don't let them turn me away without hearing and helping me!"

"Thee must come inside," a kind woman said when Belle knocked on the door. "We will help thee." Belle told her story. "Thee must spend the night." The Quaker woman gestured toward the bedroom. "Tomorrow we will drive thee to Kingston so thou may present thy case before the grand jury."

Belle stared long at the clean, white beautiful bed that night. At last she decided. It was time she slept *in* beds, not under them.

Belle jumped out of the wagon the next day and stood in front of the courthouse, staring up at the great, high dome. How would she know who to talk to? Busy white men walked back and forth. No one stopped to talk to her. One of them was dressed especially fancy, though. "Sir," she begged. "You look so grand. Are you part of the grand jury?"

The man laughed at her, but he did tell her to

walk inside the building and to the third floor. Belle had never been in such a fine building, among so many whites, but this was for her son— and God was on her side. Unable to read the signs on doors, she just kept asking men until someone told her what to do. Unable to tell time, she had no idea how to "wait fifteen minutes" in order to speak to someone. Unable to read calendars, she could not agree to come back on a particular day.

But she kept coming back time after time. Other Quakers and lawyers heard about her case and donated her legal fees. Though she was given enough to buy some clothes and shoes, Belle saved every penny for the fight to get her baby back. Again and again Belle strode into the county courthouse, until, late in 1828, Peter was brought back.

Belle held her breath as he was led into the courtroom. "Oh, my baby!" she cried. Little Peter's cheek and forehead were scarred and he looked terrified.

"That's not my mama!" Peter screamed, sobbing. Belle's heart nearly broke. What had they done to her baby?

The judge listened to the lawyers, to Peter, and

to Dr. Gedney. "I believe this truly is this woman's son," the judge finally said. "Belle Van Wagenen, you may take him. He is free."

Belle took Peter home along the dusty road that led to where she was working as a servant. When she could, she hugged him. "Ow!" he cried. Right there in the road she pulled off his shirt. He was covered with scars. He even had scars on the bottoms of his feet! "What did they do to you, baby?" Belle wailed.

Slowly Peter's story came out. Master Fowler whipped him over and over. Sometimes, bleeding, Peter would crawl under the porch. If Mistress Eliza found him, she would sneak him back into the house after everyone was asleep and grease his wounds. "It was Master Fowler that made me say you are not my mama," he said.

"Oh, Lord"—Belle called on God to curse the Fowlers—"render them double for what they have done to my baby!"

Months later Belle heard news that shook her to her soul. Mr. Fowler hadn't just been beating his powerless black slaves. He was also beating his wife—and he had finally beaten her to death. Belle realized that Eliza, even though she was white, was, in her marriage, as powerless as a slave. Belle remembered her angry prayer and was filled with horror. She had asked God to make them pay, double. And now God had answered her terrible prayer. What could she ever do to make up for causing a death?

Wicked City

"Peter," Belle told her son, "we're going to move to New York City with the Greers!"

"Not those old white people from church!" Peter whined.

"Hush your mouth! They paid me well as their housekeeper. Mrs. Greer has friends in the city who have a room for us to live in. And I have a ticket from church to get me into a New York City congregation. We'll have a good life there, son. I just know it."

After a day-long boat trip down the Hudson River, Belle and her son finally saw their new home. The city was dirty, crowded, smelly, and busier than anything Belle had ever seen.

"I love this!" Peter cried. Belle was not so sure. There were so many things she did not know. Where would she get a job, or food, or clothes and shoes, or spoons, or hairbrushes? How would she meet people in a city? Would Peter find friends? Would she? The list of things she didn't know seemed endless.

Belle found work quickly as a housekeeper. She joined the Greers' church, then switched to a church where everyone—the ministers, the deacons, the choir, and the congregation—was black. After several months she met one of her older sisters there. They wept and hugged, and Sophie told Belle that her brother lived in New York City too. Then Sophie got serious. "Nancy was here too."

"The one who got put into a box and sold?" Sophie nodded at Belle's question and went on to describe Nancy's sad end. As she spoke, Belle began weeping again. She remembered meeting Nancy and talking with her at church, but she had never known it was her own long lost sister. And now she was dead! "Oh, Lord," Belle cried, "what is this slavery that it can do such dreadful things? What evil can it not do?"

Through Mrs. Greer, Belle met friends who seemed to do nothing but good. The Latourettes had a boardinghouse where several free blacks lived. They all worked in homes and shops, factories and gardens in the city, then gathered to eat at the family table at night. The Latourettes held church services right in their "upper room." It made fitting in easy for Belle. Anyone could come to the Latourette's "free meetings." The Bible was their only text. Belle could preach whenever she felt moved to, and the room upstairs was always full of loud shouts of "Halleluja!" and "Glory!" James Latourette's group was soon known as the "Holy Club."

In the 1800s women's dress was very formal. Ladies' long, wide skirts swept the ground. Showing even an ankle was thought crude and shameful. Whenever they were outdoors, women's

hands were covered with tight white gloves. They had to keep their arms covered and they wore lacy scarves up to their necks to cover any "private" skin that might show. Only men wore pants, and no one wore shorts. Women loved ruffles and bows and fancy stitching, pleats and lace and pearl buttons.

The members of the Holy Club decided to dress plainly and against fashion, though they all earned enough money to buy fancy clothes. Belle began wearing solid, dark-colored dresses with white collars. A modest white turban kept her hair covered. At nearly six feet tall, the plain clothing made Belle look serious and very dramatic. She sang her sermons in the upper room as often as she spoke them, and her speaking voice was low and strong and full of spirit. Instead of the careful, fine words chosen by most of the people of the times, Belle used the earthy language of the farm and of slavery.

The Holy Club, like other "perfectionist" groups in the 1800s, refused to drink coffee, tea, or liquor. They often skipped meals. Just as she had while at the Dumonts, Belle drove herself extra hard to be a part of things. If the groups fasted through two meals, Belle made herself skip three. She spent more time than anybody else in the Holy Club visiting the poor, the orphans, and the sick of the wicked city, preaching wherever she went. She also preached at "camp meetings" held in tents during the summers at Sing Sing, New York.

As a slave Belle had been raised since birth to be a silent follower, obeying all orders without question. Now, in her preaching, she discovered the talent—and the yearning—to be a leader.

Black women in New York City had very few chances to lead: teaching at the new black schools, in charity work, the abolition movement, or church groups. At thirty-three, Belle still had no idea how to read or write, so she could not teach. She did not enjoy her Holy Club work among the poor as much as preaching, which came naturally to her.

Belle still spoke with a Dutch accent and in country terms. While white audiences were moved by her honest, earthy style, to many blacks she just sounded ignorant. It was an image they were working hard to shed. Most blacks left Belle's tent to go and listen to black preachers who were well-spoken, thoughtful, and educated. Belle felt alone and rejected by her own people.

Peter was no joy to her either. The scars on his face were matched by scars inside from his horrible childhood. It left him angry, rude, and cold. Belle tried over and over to find him schooling or work with friends of hers, and each time Peter failed. Belle tried to make everything better for her son, but it only got worse. Peter, tall and strong like his mother, became violent and stole things so he could buy drink and drugs.

Belle felt that Peter's city friends were wicked and a bad influence on Peter. When Peter got in trouble with the law, Belle got him freed from jail. She got him a job outside the city. He came back and got arrested again. Finally, when he was a young teenager, Belle got him work on a whaling ship. She hoped that being out at sea for a few years and away from his troublemaking friends and the city would solve his problem.

Over the next year and a half Belle got a few letters from him. Then the letters stopped coming.

Was Peter watching the stars from ports on the far side of the world? Belle never knew. She was not watching the stars herself. Belle was lonely for more than stars and memories.

She had no Master watching over her now, and never would again. Slavery was over in New York and so was the closeness of slaves forced to suffer together. There was no man in Belle's life. She allowed herself no drink, no drugs, no dancing.

Belle felt like a failure. She knew she hadn't been a good mother and she was having no success trying to preach to blacks. The only thing anybody seemed to like about her at all was how religious she was. She longed to perfect that part of herself so others would accept her.

Belle thought that Elijah Pierson, a white neighbor of the Latourettes, was the holiest person she had ever met. Several couples and other single people had moved into his big house to be part of his joyful community of faith. They called themselves the "Kingdom of God on Earth" and Belle envied the close, family feeling of the group.

Pierson's followers prayed more often than other perfectionists, saw visions, and even spoke in strange languages as the passion of their prayers loosened their tongues. When Elijah's housekeeper had to travel to visit relatives, she asked Belle to take her place. It was the chance Belle had hoped for. Now she could display her faith and her preaching, too, in a group that might welcome her.

Pierson gave her a job cooking and cleaning with the Kingdom. Belle tried hard to fit in. She fasted longer than anyone else, she prayed louder, spoke in stranger tongues, wept, preached, and shook wildly with "the Spirit"—besides cooking, sewing, and cleaning for the whole Pierson household. To her joy, Elijah and the other dozen members of the Kingdom let her know she—and her labor—were important. Belle belonged!

One day she answered the Pierson's door to see a young-looking white man with shoulder-length hair and a long beard. Belle's first thought was that he looked like Jesus. Shaggy Robert Matthias had heard of Pierson and the Kingdom of God group and felt called to come to them. He spoke so well and earnestly about how he could heal the sick, forgive sins, and punish the wicked, that Belle— and Pierson, too—believed him. Within days he had moved into the Piersons' house.

Matthias never told the Kingdom about the wife and children he had left behind. He never mentioned how often he had been arrested for barging into churches and pushing the preachers out of the way. "I am Christ," he tried to tell the police who dragged him away again and again. He was not violent, so they had to let him go wandering again, looking for people who would believe him.

The Kingdom was ready to believe. They worshipped Matthias, obeying his every command to prove their religious faith. Belle was kept too busy downstairs cooking in the kitchen, washing sheets and curtains, and preparing feasts to be part of all the wonderfully joyous "worship" that was going on upstairs. She believed all of Matthias's fine words— because he told her to. And everybody else seemed to believe him as well. She was not allowed to preach, since Matthias thought it was wrong for women to preach. It was almost like being back in her life at the Dumonts. Now when she remembered that part of her life she thought about the beatings and the abuse, but she also remembered being needed, working hard, obeying without question, being part of something big, being loved. It was the only kind of happy she had ever known.

Matthias even whipped his followers when they were not obedient. He did not ask to be called "Master." Instead everyone had to call him "Father." He sat at the head of the table and made strict rules about everyone's behavior. Matthias talked his followers into giving him their money and property, too.

One of the men owned a house on the river at Sing Sing. Matthias and Pierson would charter a steamboat and take their entire Kingdom— including Belle to cook and clean—up to this summer home. They hired other black servants, but Belle was the only black to eat at their table. They needed and valued her, and that was all that mattered to Belle.

✿ ✿ ✿

It all came to an end when Pierson died unexpectedly. He had been ill, but his relatives and friends questioned just how sick he really had been. They wondered about where all of his money had gone. They questioned what, exactly, all those people had been doing in that house. It was a cult, they said. Pierson and Matthias had been fighting in the house. Matthias was accused of murdering his partner, and he was arrested.

During the investigation Belle heard for the first time about all the strange things that had been going on upstairs while she was hard at work: trading wives, group baths, "religious" beatings. Every juicy detail of the cult was spread across the front pages of the *New York Times* and other newspapers. The reporters said Belle was in on the baths, the murder, the sex. She was horrified. Matthias was freed, but Belle's faith was deeply shaken.

Just when it seemed all the hurt and sorrow was over, Benjamin Folger, a Kingdom member, wrote a novel about life with Matthias. It was full of half-truths and lies. It repeated all the worst parts of the newspaper stories, but it also said that Belle had killed Pierson.

It was only a book, but everyone was reading it. Everyone was beginning to think that Belle was the one who started the strange ceremonies and poisoned Pierson. How could she fight against thousands of copies of the book?

Belle decided to use the law again—this time to protect her honor. She sued Benjamin Folger for libel, the saying of hurtful lies against someone. Belle, still illiterate and uneducated, still a black woman in a white man's world, won that case.

Belle realized that she had become a kind of slave again. She had traded her freedom for the hope of belonging. At first she had simply been foolish, believing too easily. Then the joy of belonging had blinded her to what was really happening in the cult. In the end she had made herself believe all was well, even when she had begun to doubt Matthias and Pierson. Belle decided she would never again let anyone be the master of her body—or her mind.

But what else was there for her to do?

The Sojourn Begins

"That's *all* the money I have, sir?" Belle stood in the crowded bank lobby. The man behind the iron bars nodded. "You are sure?" she asked. She had been working hard as a housekeeper for so many years!

"See for yourself," he said, and turned the book. "June 1, 1843," he read aloud for her. "And here is your total." Belle looked blankly at the pencil scribbles on the page, then turned and wandered out onto the busy sidewalk.

All the money she'd given to the Kingdom was gone of course. Matthias had taken everything with him when he went out west after his trial. The lawyer for her own libel case had cost a lot, but all the evil lies had been cleared from her name. "Belle Van Wagenen" meant something good again. Belle stood still and watched couples hurrying by, the men in top hats and vests, the women holding their skirts up from the filth on the ground. Boys in short knickers chased a hoop, tapping it with a stick. No one looked at her. Belle stood frozen. Her name was clear, but who was she now that it was all over?

Nobody nice, that was for sure, Belle thought. She listed her failures. She was foolish enough to believe in the crooks leading a cult. She had left her daughters behind, and sent her only son off to vanish at sea. And she didn't do good for anyone. Belle remembered the time her employer had given her a half dollar to hire a poor man to clean the new-fallen snow from his front steps. "I'll see to it, sir," she had said, then shoveled the snow and tucked the coin into her own apron pocket.

Later that very morning a homeless man had stood on the step, his hat in his hand. "I sure hope there's work for me today, sister. My chillun, they is hungry." And Belle had just shaken her head no

90

at the man. She had taken work from him, just like work had been taken from her since she came to New York City. Belle looked around her. She tried to think of anything good that had happened in the wicked city.

My preaching. She nodded to herself. That was good. But the city was bad. Things were coming clear to her, and she began walking, praying silently. By the time she reached the little room she rented, her mind was made up. She would spend the rest of her life doing the only thing she was really good at. God had given her the gift to touch people with her voice.

Belle hurried up the stairs and threw the few clothes she might need into her pillowcase and tossed what food she had into a basket.

"What are you doing, Belle?" her landlady asked through the open door.

"I'm leaving, Mrs. Whiting." Belle looked into her little purse, then pulled the drawstrings shut firmly.

"When?" the woman gasped. "Now? Do your children know?"

"It would only worry them," Belle said, "and my

name is no longer Belle. Now I am a sojourner." It sounded so good spoken out loud. "I am Sojourner," she repeated the new name. "I am going to wander to the east and preach."

"The east?" Mrs. Whiting shook her head. "What are you going east for?"

"The Spirit calls me there and I must go." Belle stood up and looked out the window. The early June sunshine bathed the grimy cityscape with a warm glow. With a smile, Sojourner left.

The sunshine warmed her face as she rode the ferry to Brooklyn. Light flooded the yards of the homes she wandered past. Sojourner did not let herself look back at the city, or her decision to leave it. One moment's look back had stopped Lot's wife as she left the wicked city of Sodom. Nothing was going to stop Sojourner. Her legs quickly remembered how long strides ate up country miles. She breathed deeply as she swung along the road. The air here was so clean!

At midday Sojourner sat on a mossy bank beside the road and chewed at some of the cheese she'd brought along. A carriage passed, and then a wagon. People nodded to her from horseback. Sojourner finished her lunch with water from a nearby stream and she was on her way again.

As evening fell Sojourner began wondering how God would provide her a place to stay. A stranger walked out onto the road and asked her if she needed work. "I'm on my way to do the Lord's work," she told him. He asked her to come home with him. His wife was very sick. God, Sojourner thought, had meant for her to be on that very road at the moment the man was searching for help. She spent several weeks helping with chores in his home, but she felt a greater calling to preach. When the man's wife was well enough, Sojourner headed out onto the road again, taking only twenty-five cents as thanks for countless hours of work. "Don't need money," she told the Quaker man. "God will provide."

When the afternoon sun became hot she began knocking on doors, looking for a place to stay and a drink of fresh water.

"What is thy name, sister?" a Quaker housewife asked.

"Sojourner," she answered. The housewife paused, waiting to hear her last name too. Sojourner didn't know which last name to tell her. Hardenbergh? Neely? Schryver? Dumont? Van Wagenen? Those names just showed who had owned her. What name would *she* use for herself? The answer took forty-six-year-old Sojourner's breath away: She had a new Master now—God . . . the God of truth. She took a deep breath and named herself.

"My name is Sojourner Truth," she told the housewife, "because from this day I will walk in the light of His truth."

"Come in."

Sojourner was not welcomed into every place she stopped for the night, but many homes opened their doors to her. Wandering preachers were an interesting change from the everyday boredom of farm life. An evangelist ready to preach the gospel was a reason to invite the neighbors in for an

evening's sermon and hymn sing. These travelers gave everyone something to talk about for months afterward, and sometimes these evangelists were truly inspiring. Sojourner, a gaunt, tall figure with her strange voice full of passion, promised to be more entertaining than most.

She was, in fact, much more than entertaining. "I speaks to God, and God speaks to me," she began at the first outdoor religious meeting she attended. The crowd murmured. They were not used to hearing from a black person, but Sojourner won them over. At the Kingdom group Matthias had said women could not preach. Belle had stayed silent, but she had listened carefully to all the tricks the cult leader had used to make people believe and obey him. Now what Matthias had been using for evil, Sojourner used for God. Her listeners believed. They told their friends.

People flocked to camp meetings where Sojourner was to speak. Posters were spread about the towns she would be visiting. A huge tent was set up. Tables groaned under the food that local people brought. There was dancing, feasting, singing, and the joy of God—just like at the exciting Pinkster celebrations of Sojourner's youth.

She went from meeting to meeting, out on Long Island, across Long Island Sound to Connecticut, inland to New Haven, and on north to Springfield, Massachusetts. Along the way she stopped to have letters written to her children to tell them that she was safe and doing God's work. Friends in Springfield told her about the Northampton Society, a group of people living and working together in equality and Christian fellowship. They lived together in a huge old factory. They raised caterpillars and used the cocoons to create silk cloth. Sojourner didn't trust them at first. Was this a cult like Matthias's Kingdom? She would not let herself be fooled twice, but she agreed to visit.

Many of the people there were smart and famous. Well-known white abolitionists like Wendell Phillips and Parker Pillsbury lived in the community. An old black abolitionist friend of Sojourner's, David Ruggles, was part of the commune too. He had helped six hundred slaves along on the Underground Railroad toward safety in the North. Frederick Douglass, a famous runaway slave twenty years younger than Sojourner, often visited the society. He had learned to read, and wrote for the *North Star*, an antislavery newspaper. His book, *Narrative of the Life of Frederick Douglass, an American Slave*, was sold all over the North. It was often smuggled into the slaveholding South, too, and it was turning ever more people against slavery.

Not everyone at the Northampton Society was famous, but whoever they were, white or black, the men and women lived together in equality. Like members of the Kingdom, they and their children ate together, shared all work and money, and felt that everyone should live the same as they did. But this Northampton Society had no "Father" or all-powerful leader like Matthias. There were no beatings. There were no strange ceremonies, either. Everyone didn't have to believe the same thing. Sojourner made sure of that before she decided to work within the society.

＊ ＊ ＊

One of Sojourner's new friends in Northampton was a white woman, Olive Gilbert. She read Douglass's book aloud to Sojourner. She also read Garrison's abolitionist newspaper, the *Liberator,* to her. Sojourner memorized the words as she had when the Bible had been read and was able to remember exact quotes to use in her speeches. Sojourner heard that some black abolitionists wanted the slaves to rise up and attack their owners. A war between the slaveholding states and the free ones seemed possible. Garrison and Douglass argued in the press against violence. Sojourner knew God would want to avoid bloodshed—but surely all slaves should be free!

Members of the community talked over these and other ideas during meals and while picking silk cocoons from the huge trays of caterpillars. While spreading mulberry leaves on the trays for the caterpillars to eat, the society members talked. They argued in the lettuce patch and chatted while doing the dishes. Ideas flowed like silk threads through the factory and everyone took part in the

discussions: famous abolitionists, college profes-
sors, doctors, and Sojourner.

Now and then Sojourner went out to preach at camp
meetings. She was so open and honest that one day
someone asked "What is it like to be a slave?"
Sojourner paused. She was there to spread God's
word, not her own story. She knew that she was not
well-spoken like Frederick Douglass. Her failure
with black crowds in New York still stung. But this
was a crowd of whites, and they seemed friendly.

So Sojourner prayed for help loudly. Then she
sang a hymn. Finally she began, "Children, slavery
is an evil thing." She took another breath. "They
sell children away from their mothers, then dare
the mothers to cry." The audience sat hushed and
leaned forward. "What manner of men can do
these things?" Sojourner went on, telling them
about being beaten . . . about sleeping in the mud
of a cellar hole . . . about having her brothers and
sisters sold away . . . about being sold with a flock
of sheep. There were so many stories!

Her audience grew angry. "Them abolitionists

was right!" a farmer muttered. "Slavery is just as bad as they said. It has to end!"

Sojourner's breath caught in her throat. Could her voice help the millions of slaves still being held in the South? The answer came to her as strong as a message from God Himself. This was something she *had* to do—to work to end human suffering.

Her antislavery messages were not always welcomed. At one camp meeting near Northampton a mob of young men carrying clubs and sticks interrupted her speech. The local people ran screaming. The evangelists sprinted for safety. Sojourner ran and hid. As she sat there trembling, anger began to grow. "Shall I run away from the Devil?" she thought. "If I go out there, the Lord will protect me."

Sojourner stood up, feeling as if she had three hearts that were so large her body could barely hold them. Alone, she walked out away from the tent to a nearby rise. She stood on that little hilltop and began to sing, her voice loud enough to get the mob's attention. When they ran toward her, she didn't run. One of them spread his arms to stop the others. "Keep singing, old woman," he demanded. "Tell us your stories."

Calmly Sojourner took control of the crowd. She raised her voice, speaking and singing, making them laugh and making them think. For hours she answered their questions and sang for them. Finally she stopped. "I have a request to make of you," she said. "Will you leave in peace if I sing you one more song?" Amazed by her bravery and touched by her words, the men agreed. After that song, they left quietly. The camp meeting went on—and so did Sojourner.

Back at the silk mill Olive was talking about another issue: women's rights. Women were almost like slaves to their husbands in the 1800s. The men owned the money, the property, and the children. If a wife was beaten, there was nothing she could do about it. Sojourner knew all about that. It was how poor Eliza Fowler had died in the South. If there was a divorce, a woman lost everything. A woman could not be a mayor or a senator, or hold any public office. She could not be on a jury. She could not be a judge, a policeman, or a minister. Those were the laws. They were not fair, but there was nothing women could do about it. Or was there?

Women could not vote. That meant they could not vote to change the laws. And they could not vote to elect people—perhaps even women—to political office. Only white men could vote, and they did not want to give up that power.

Sojourner agreed with Olive, but reminded her friend that it was even worse for black free women—and it was worst of all for slave women. Slaves were treated badly by their Masters and Mistresses *and* often by their husbands, too. Perhaps, Sojourner thought, she could do something about that? Winning equal rights for women became part of her speeches too.

While she was with the Northampton Society, Sojourner invited her daughters to come and live with her. Anyone who was willing to work in the community was given a clean bed in the huge dormitory upstairs in the factory building, clothes to wear, and food. It was a wonderful life, but the silk wasn't selling well. The news from the country wasn't good, either.

More and more slaves were escaping from the states near the North. Some sneaked away on their own. Many were helped by the Underground Railroad: Free blacks, slaves, and whites hid runaway slaves in their homes along the way to free states and gave them rides, shoes, clothes, and money. One famous slave, Harriet Tubman, ran away and made it safely to the free state of Pennsylvania. Instead of staying there, she risked her life again and again to sneak back into slave-holding states and lead other slaves to freedom.

The slave Masters were furious. They paid men to catch the runaways. Horrible stories of the killings and tortures by these slave hunters and the punishments Masters gave to runaways who were caught filled the *North Star,* the *Liberator,* and the society's dinner-table conversations.

"You should write a book of your life like Frederick Douglass's," Olive said to Sojourner one day.

"You know I cain't write nor read." Sojourner barely looked up from her sewing.

Olive put her own needle down. "You could tell me what to write, dear. I'll wager that William Garrison would publish your story, too. We could sell it everywhere. Imagine what good your words would do for the cause!"

Garrison was happy to put up the money for *Narrative of Sojourner Truth: A Northern Slave.* There was already a book about Harriet Tubman helping the slaves escape from the South along the Underground Railroad. Frederick Douglass had been a slave in the South. There were other books about the evils of slavery in the South. All those books made northerners think that only southern Masters would do evil things to slaves. Sojourner's book told them the truth.

In 1850 her story was published. Once Garrison's money was paid back, Sojourner got to keep a little money from each copy sold. Now she needed the money. The Northampton Society was closing down. The silk business failed and everyone had to leave. Sojourner was fifty-three. Where would she go?

William Garrison loaned her three hundred dollars to buy a house in Northampton. He knew the money would keep coming in from the sale of her book and from the money she was now paid as a speaker at abolition meetings.

Now there was more reason to speak than ever. A new law called the "Fugitive Slave Act" meant that any escaped slave could be chased down anywhere in the U.S., no matter how long that slave had been at large, and returned to the horrors of slavery. The Underground Railroad got longer. Now runaways had to sneak all the way to Canada for safety—and freedom. Frederick Douglass fled to England. Friends there finally bought his freedom from his angry owner.

Many people were horrified when their neighbors—good, hard-working people—were carried away. The abolitionists gained support daily, but only in the North.

Southern farmers needed slaves. They depended on them to work in their fields, their huge homes, their factories, and their shops. It was a state's right to allow slavery if it wanted, they argued. As new states were added to the country, battles were fought to keep the number of slave states and free states even. For now they were mostly battles of words and fists. But blood was shed when an abolitionist named John Brown led an attack on slaveholders in Kansas.

Sojourner's voice was her weapon against slavery. "Well, children," she began one speech, "I was born a slave in Ulster County, New York. I don't know if it was summer or winter, fall or spring. I don't even know what day of the week it was. They don't care when a slave is born. . . ." She talked about her own father, Baumfree, dying alone in a shed. She explained how hard she'd fought to get little Peter back, and how horribly scarred he was. Sojourner closed with, "God will not make his face to shine upon a nation that holds with slavery!"

Many people sobbed at her words. Others sat stunned into silence. Still others cheered wildly. Sojourner made up words to go with tunes everyone knew. To the tune of "Auld Lang Syne," Sojourner's deep voice rang out:

"I am pleading for my people,
A poor, downtrodden race,
Who dwell in freedom's boasted land,
With no abiding place.
I am pleading for the mothers
Who gaze in wild despair
Upon the hated auction block,
And see their children there."

People sang along, reading the words from song sheets Sojourner sold for a nickel or a dime. Dozens of her books sold at each of her speeches too, and Sojourner's fame spread. She spoke out against slavery over and over, in tent meetings, in churches, in parlors, and on street corners throughout New England.

In 1850 she was invited to speak at the first National Women's Conference in Worcester, Massachusetts. A thousand people from eleven states came to talk about women's rights. Newspapers, written by men, made fun of the women. Preachers, all of whom were men, said the women were doing the devil's work. Some even swore that no woman who went to the conference could ever enter their church again.

Sojourner was the only black speaker. She listened to the rich white women arguing for the right to keep their jewelry if they got divorced. She smiled with amusement when the women talked about being able, for once, to wear pants instead of long skirts. That seemed a silly argument. When she was a slave, Sojourner had tucked her skirts up into her belt whenever she needed to. A young school-teacher, Lucretia Mott, complained about being paid less than a male teacher, just because she was a woman. Sojourner found that a worthy argument. Another speaker, Lucy Stone, told the group that she was not using her husband's last name. "He is not my Master!" Sojourner understood that.

These issues were all important to her, but she had little patience with the chatter. "Sisters," she said when she finally got a chance, "I'm not clear what you be after. If women want more rights than they've got, why don't they just take them and not be talking about it!"

Equality before the law was the group's final demand, without distinction of sex or color.

Letters from home reached her as she traveled. Friends read aloud to Sojourner that Elizabeth and Diana had married. She had grandchildren! John Dumont had had become an abolitionist and gone west with one of his sons. Sojourner missed her old friends and family, but she felt she needed to keep traveling to do the Lord's work.

First she stopped to visit with Harriet Beecher Stowe, the author of *Uncle Tom's Cabin*. This powerful little book about the horrible life of a slave family had already sold two million copies. Harriet wrote it after the Fugitive Slave Act was passed, and its sad story had moved everyone who read it to tears—and to the abolition cause. Words, spoken and written, were fanning the anger of a divided country.

Sojourner took her message west to Ohio. Here the crowds were often unfriendly. She had to yell over the hisses and boos of proslavery protesters. "I see," she said to them, "that some of you have got the spirit of a goose and some of you have the spirit of a snake!" The crowds weren't any better at a Women's Rights Convention in Akron. Even the people who set up the convention did not want her to speak. This meeting wasn't about slavery. What could she say to help fight for women's equality here?

"Well, children," she said, when she finally got the chance, "that man over there"—she pointed to a minister—"he said women are the weaker sex. He says women need to be helped into carriages and lifted over ditches and to have the best treatment everywhere." She paused. "Nobody *ever* helps me into carriages, over mud puddles, or gets me any best places. . . ." She stood tall, loud, and proud, saying, "And ain't *I* a woman?"

"Look at me!" She pulled her right arm out of its sleeve and everyone gasped at the sight of its nakedness. From years of labor, muscles bulged beneath her dark skin. "I have ploughed. And I have planted. And I have gathered into barns. And no man could head me." She stared around the room and whispered, "And ain't *I* a woman?

"I have borne children and seen them sold into slavery, and when I cried out a mother's grief, none but Jesus heard me." She stared right at the ministers. "You say Jesus was a man so that means God favors men over women? Where did your Christ come from?"

She paused and repeated, "Where did your Christ come from?" She answered herself slowly. "From God and a woman. Man had nothing to do with him."

Carrying six hundred copies of her book, Sojourner crisscrossed Ohio, speaking to crowds who did not care for her ideas. "I don't care any more for your talk," a farmer yelled at her, "than I do for the bite of a flea!"

Sojourner just laughed at him. "Lord willing," she said, "I'll keep you scratchin'." She kept on traveling throughout Ohio and Indiana, preaching and singing and lecturing, giving them all something to think about. By 1857 Sojourner was sixty and ready to stop her life on the road. She sold her house in Northampton for $750 and moved to the

Harmonia colony near Battle Creek, Michigan. Many people who believed in equality and abolition already lived there. By 1860 her daughter Diana moved there too, with her husband and son, Frank. Elizabeth also moved to Harmonia with her son, Sammy. The little boy, so like Peter, asked if he could live with his grandmother. Sammy helped her with errands and chores, listened to her tales, and when he learned to read, he read the Bible to her.

But Sojourner was not cut out to be a grand-mother, rocking her life away on a quiet front porch. She soon planned another speaking tour, this time through Indiana. She took Sammy with her and sold copies of her book, her songs, and souvenir photos of herself to raise money for expenses. "I sell the shadow," the photos said, "to support the substance."

Indiana was even more challenging than Ohio. "We'll burn down the hall where you are going to speak," a man threatened.

"Very well," Sojourner said calmly. "I'll speak on the ashes."

In one church where Sojourner was speaking, a

113

proslavery group claimed that she was a fraud. "We demand," the leader of the group said, "that if it be a she, that she show her breast to the gaze of some of the ladies present." The ladies then, he said, would report back to the roomful of listeners.

"Why do you think me a man?" Sojourner challenged him.

He said her voice was "not the voice of a woman."

Sojourner thought quickly. He was only trying to embarrass her. How many times had she shown her breasts to a roomful of whites while she nursed her Master's babies? Sojourner began unbuttoning her blouse.

"I will show my breast to the entire congregation," she said. "It is not my shame, but yours that I do this." Then she pulled her blouse open wide. The proper Victorian men gasped with embarrassment. The prim ladies blushed and covered their eyes or reached for their smelling salts. Sojourner calmly closed her shirt and went on with her speech.

Any calm left in the country was fading. In October of 1859, John Brown attacked again. He tried to get slaves to revolt, starting with those living near the armory at Harpers Ferry, Virginia. A handful of men were killed. Brown was caught, tried, and hanged; but the damage was done. People everywhere were singing "John Brown's body lies a mouldering in the grave, but his soul goes marching on." In the slave states, there were three times as many slaves as masters. The owners were terrified that another uprising would kill them all if their slaves followed John Brown's lead. They became even more brutal in order to keep their slaves scared and helpless.

Sammy read the papers to Sojourner, now back in Michigan.

Abraham Lincoln, a young abolitionist, ran for president in the fall of 1860. He won. Seven southern states left the United States in protest. Four more left after a rebel general fired on Fort Sumter on April 12, 1861. The slave-owning states created a new nation, called the Confederate States of America, and the Civil War began.

War

"Let me get my hat." Sojourner's answer came quickly when a friend invited her on another speaking tour of Indiana. It meant leaving her comfortable home in Battle Creek. It meant facing angry crowds again. It meant forcing her sixty-five-year-old body back into action. But Sojourner did not hesitate. Like blacks throughout the country, Sojourner was ready to do anything to help end slavery.

Battles were being fought with bullets now, not just voices. "You can be a cook for the army," black men were told when they tried to join the fight, or, "You can work in the hospital tents." In the early days of the war, they could not carry guns in the U.S. Army. Most white officers had never known a black person, or had a black friend. They did not know if they would fight—or run—under fire. Would a black soldier save a white one on a battlefield? Would whites fight to save a black comrade?

Finally, in 1862, Lincoln ordered the U.S. Army to form a regiment of black soldiers. The Fifty-fourth Massachusetts Volunteer Infantry was only a "test," and it included white officers. Blacks from around the country made their way to Boston to enlist. One of Sojourner's grandsons volunteered, along with two of Frederick Douglass's sons. The men of the Fifty-fourth fought like heroes.

Dreadful, bloody battles were fought between the Union army of the United States and the Confederate States' troops. It was hard to tell who was winning, but it was easy to tell who was dying. Hundreds of thousands of young men from farms and towns across the country were losing their lives on battlefields. And the war went on.

✳ ✳ ✳ ✳

The abolitionists were restless. When would Lincoln announce the end of slavery? Trained as a lawyer, Lincoln had always said slaves should be emancipated, giving them their freedom legally and forever. Sojourner understood what he was waiting for. When she was speaking, it always took her a while to get the sense of a crowd. She had to use all of her tricks to get everyone on her side before she could ask them to change their lives.

"Children, have patience!" she scolded people who said the president should hurry. "It takes a while to turn about this great ship of state."

Finally on January 1, 1863, President Lincoln signed the order freeing all slaves "thenceforward and forever." To celebrate the Emancipation Proclamation parties were held everywhere in the North. Church bells rang in every steeple. People gathered in the streets, singing and dancing. It was like a huge Pinkster celebration spread over the twenty-four states left in the United States of America.

❄ ❄ ❄ ❄

A few weeks later, Sojourner had a stroke. The blood vessel that had broken in her brain left her weak and confused for a time. Though she was healing, rumors flew that the great Sojourner Truth had died. Newspapers and magazines wrote about her death. Harriet Beecher Stowe wrote a beautiful article about Sojourner's life, calling her "The Libyan Sibyl." "Libyan" because Sojourner's skin was as black as the blackest African from Libya. A "sibyl" was an ancient mythic woman who could see into the future and tell what would happen. Harriet mourned that Sojourner had "passed away from among us, as a wave of the sea." Sojourner was surprised to hear this.

While the entire country read the article about poor, dead Sojourner, friends and family nursed her back to health. Her grandson Sammy did everything he could to help. One of the first things she did when her strength came back was have Sammy write a thank-you note to a surprised Ms. Stowe.

The Libyan Sibyl was not happy lying in bed or sitting in her rocking chair, smoking her clay pipe. "There's a war going on," she fretted. "And I mean to be a part of it!" Young black men from Michigan were enlisting in the new First Michigan Infantry. They were stationed near Detroit, so Sojourner went there bringing a Thanksgiving feast to the troops.

She entertained them with a song she made up to the tune of "John Brown's Body":

> *"We are the valiant soldiers who 'listed*
> *for the war;*
> *We are fighting for the union, we are*
> *fighting for the law.*
> *We can shoot a rebel farther than a white*
> *man ever saw,*
> *As we go marching on."*

She had heard that black soldiers were paid less than white ones. As always, Sojourner fought for equality with her voice, by singing:

> *"They will have to pay us wages, the*
> *wages of their sin;*
> *They will have to bow their foreheads*

to their colored kith and kin;
They will have to give us houseroom, or
   the roof will tumble in,
As we go marching on."

The war ground on for years. Sammy read the newspapers to Sojourner so she would know what was happening. As her strength came back, Sojourner went to work as a housekeeper for a few families in Battle Creek to earn money. As she worked she prayed—and made plans. "I've got to hurry with this washing," she said one day. "I'm leaving for Washington this afternoon. I'm going down there to advise the president."

This was not as easy as she had hoped. Because of the war Washington was crowded and busy. While they waited to see the president, Sojourner and Sammy found a place where their help was needed: A Freedman's Village had been set up outside the capital by the government for the freed slaves who streamed out of the South.

Sojourner understood their problems. They had no homes. They had no skills. They, like the young

slave Belle, knew nothing but beatings and obedi-
ence. Belle's struggles to find a way on her own had
led her into a cult. These new ex-slaves needed to
know everything Sojourner had learned: how to
sew, how to clean, how to find jobs and manage
money, and how to care for their children.

She even showed the poor black women how to
use the law to force whites into honesty and fair-
ness. Raiders from the South had stolen some of
the children of the village, and taken them back to
slavery. Sojourner went with the mothers to court.
They won extra protection. Now it was law. "If you
try anything like that," Sojourner warned anyone
else who might think freedmen's children were
just slaves ready for the taking, "I shall make the
United States rock like a cradle!" Sojourner had
shown the mothers how to use the legal system.
Within weeks, the courts made sure that all of the
stolen children were returned. The raids stopped.

At last Sojourner got to see the president. Instead
of looking strong and noble as she had expected,
Abraham Lincoln looked sad and tired. He stood

up, though, when she entered the room. That was a sign of respect men made to women, but usually not to blacks. Sojourner didn't have the heart to lecture him the way she had planned about how much more he ought to be doing.

Instead she told him he was like Daniel, the Bible hero, in the lion's den. Lincoln showed her a huge Bible he kept in his office, a gift from a group of blacks in Baltimore. It had fancy gold lettering on the cover. Gently touching the letters she still could not read, Sojourner reminded Lincoln that God was on his side. Like Daniel, he—and the country—would survive.

Then she told him he was the best president the United States had ever had.

Lincoln shook his head. He told her that Washington, Jefferson, and Adams were the greatest.

"They may have been good to others"—Sojourner's voice rose as she spoke—"but they neglected to do anything for my race. Washington had a good name," she went on, "but his name didn't reach to us."

Lincoln was not convinced, but Sojourner knew

this great, tired man had risked the whole country for the freedom of black slaves. The president told her she must visit him again. Before she left, she asked him to sign the autograph book she carried everywhere.

"For Aunty Sojourner Truth," he wrote, using a term of affection.

Six months later, on April 9, 1865, the Confederate Army surrendered. The war was over. The parties of celebration held tears of both relief and sadness. Slavery was gone from the country forever, but the battles had destroyed thousands of roads and railroads, homes and towns. The United Stated was united again, but half a million teenage boys and men were dead. Nearly everyone had lost brothers, sons, cousins, or a father. They all needed to celebrate. They also needed to grieve.

Five days later Lincoln was shot.

"The Great Emancipator is dead!" The news spread through Washington the next morning, on a day gray with icy drizzle and horror. Like most everyone, Sojourner stumbled about in shock. It couldn't be true! An actor, John Wilkes Booth, couldn't have killed the greatest president! But Abraham Lincoln, the kind, sad man who had freed six million slaves, was dead.

The Fight Goes On

The vice president, Andrew Johnson, was quickly sworn in as the new president. Johnson was from Tennessee, where many people had held slaves. Sojourner had to trust that he would follow the new laws of the reunited states. Blacks in Freedman's Village were terrified that they would have to be slaves again now that Lincoln was gone. Sojourner gave long, hopeful speeches to the frightened blacks there.

She felt she had to see this new president, to tell him what she had seen in the village and how important it was that the government take care of all the slaves they had set free.

"Please be seated, Mrs. Truth," President Johnson said to her from his desk chair.

Mrs. Truth? Sojourner's jaw tightened. This man had no idea who she was! He only thought of her as someone's wife. Would he ever listen to anything she had to say? She had to make him take her seriously!

"Sit down yourself, Mr. President," she said firmly. "I'm used to standing because I've been lecturing for many years." She told him of the problems of freed slaves, from her own experience and the people she knew at Freedman's Village. She had some ideas, too, of how to solve the problems.

The president listened. He didn't discuss any thing with her. He didn't answer her challenges. He didn't say anything except a final, "Thank you, Mrs. Truth."

Sojourner left without even asking him to sign her autograph book.

There was work to do, and it was clear that President Johnson wasn't going to be much help.

"Lord," she had complained years before, "I'm too old to work. I'm too sick to hold meetings and talk to people and sell my books." But now, at seventy, Sojourner took a job working in a government hospital for freed slaves. Part of the time she preached. Part of the time she nursed sick patients. And part of the time she simply strode the halls, telling blacks who had no idea how to use soap, "Be clean! Be clean!" The hospital brought her in touch with ex-slaves who were not lucky enough to be settled into Freedman's Village.

No one had planned for the number of freed slaves pouring out of the South. The village quickly filled up. Thousands of other black refugees just put up rickety shacks anywhere there was space. All they had was hope. There was no clean water, no plumbing, no schools, no jobs. Hungry, crowded, and desperate, they did whatever they could to keep their families alive. These slums earned names like "Murder Bay." They were frightening for everyone.

Sojourner worked to find homes for as many of them as she could. Some she took back to

Rochester, New York. She found work for them with her friends there. But there were too many to help each one personally.

What would happen to them all? Sojourner knew that the only real job skills field slaves had were plowing and planting. She remembered a time when she was beaten for having her own ideas about things. It taught her not to think for herself. The thoughts of a black slave, she said, "were no longer than my finger." She told everyone that it would be "quicker to learn a hog to dance than to teach field hands to sew." But if these blacks were given land, they surely could support themselves as farmers! For a while the government talked of breaking up the huge old plantations of the South. Each slave family could have some of the land that they and their parents had worked on all their lives.

Congressmen from southern states defeated that idea. Sojourner began urging people to give blacks some of the empty land out west. "Twenty acres and a mule," she argued. It was only fair. That way the slaves could be repaid for giving a life's work to the white masters.

* * * *

Sojourner's hospital job paid enough for her to live on. To save money, she walked to work most of the time. One day she decided to ride one of the horsedrawn streetcars. She stood by the curb in a spot where the cars were supposed to stop.

Three streetcars drove right past before Sojourner realized what was happening. They were passing her by because she was black. "I want to ride!" she yelled, her deep, loud voice carrying up and down the street. "Stop! I want to ride! *I want to ride!*"

Wagon drivers slowed their horses to stare at the old woman with the booming voice. Carriages hurried by or stopped. The next streetcar got caught in the traffic jam Sojourner had created. She paid no attention to the driver's threats. Instead she just climbed on board while he cursed her. "You go sit at the back," he finally snarled, "with the other blacks."

Sojourner dropped her coins into the fare box and strode to the back, filled with a cold fury. The new Jim Crow rules kept blacks and whites separate in streetcars, hotels, parks, and even at water fountains. Jim Crow was a white man who had performed a dance act on stage with his face painted black. His act was an insult to blacks, but the laws named after him were worse. They seemed to be everywhere now, shutting blacks out. Sojourner spoke out against the laws, but she did more.

One day Sojourner waited for a streetcar with Laura Haviland, a white friend. As the car came near, Sojourner stood aside while Laura waved. The driver stopped to pick Laura up, but she let Sojourner jump aboard first.

"Get out of the way," the conductor yelled, pushing at her, "and let this lady come in."

"Whoop!" Sojourner answered. "Well, I am a lady too!" And she sat down. After a few stops both women had to change cars to get where they were going. Again Laura got the streetcar to stop.

"Are niggers allowed to ride?" a passenger asked loudly on his way down the steps.

The conductor grabbed Sojourner by the shoulder and told her to leave. Laura grabbed her other arm and pulled her aboard instead. "Does she

belong to you?" the conductor challenged.

"No," Laura said, looking him in the eye. "She belongs to humanity."

His face got red. "Then take her and go!" he said, and slammed Sojourner against the streetcar door hard enough to dislocate her shoulder.

Sojourner used the law again. She took the case to court, charging the conductor with assault and battery. She won and the driver lost his job. It was a warning to all of the drivers in the Washington area. They knew now they could not just grab black riders and throw them off their streetcars. "Before the trial was ended," Sojourner bragged, "the insides of the cars looked like pepper and salt."

The Libyan Sibyl gave speeches everywhere about blacks getting the right to vote. In 1870 the future she foretold came true. The Fifteenth Amendment to the U.S. Constitution was finally passed. Black citizens could vote.

But women were not full citizens. They still could not vote. They had no rights.

Women everywhere were furious. Women abolitionists were especially angry. They had worked for
years for freedom for blacks and women—and the
law was still in the hands of the men in power.

As she had with the streetcar rules, Sojourner
challenged this new, unfair law. "We need women
lawyers, women judges, women on juries, and
women in Congress," she said. The men laughed
and paid no attention.

The Fourteenth Amendment of 1868 gave black
men equal power and protections under the law.
Some white men were threatened by this new
legal equality. They wanted their power back.
They had liked being in charge and wanted things
to stay that way. All of the ex-slaves were out looking for jobs now too. That meant they were com-
peting with white men—but slaves were used to
working for nothing. They were happy to work for
low wages. Often white men found themselves out
of work. They were angry at the changes in their
lives. The anger came out in many ways.

The new Jim Crow laws put blacks "back in their

places." Violence against blacks increased. Men who were used to beating slaves whenever the mood struck them lashed out in their anger now. Worse still, a secret cult had formed in the South. Calling themselves the Imperial Order of the Ku Klux Klan, the Klansmen swore to take control back by terrorizing the blacks in their communities.

They wore white hoods to hide their faces and long cloaks that hid their bodies so they could not be identified. Too cowardly to show themselves, they took the law into their own hands, shooting and hanging blacks in their communities and burning black people's homes. Sometimes they left wooden crosses burning in their yards as if terrorism was a Christian act. What they did was against the law, but often policemen and judges were Klansmen too. Branches of this cult spread here and there around the country, wherever white men's anger overflowed into pure evil.

At the same time good people everywhere were working hard, knitting their neighborhoods back together. They fought for law and order and peace in their towns, rebuilt roads and schools, and replanted fields. New babies were born, new businesses started, and new states settled. It was an uneasy time. Everyone had hoped that things would be fine after the war. Four long years of war were over, but no one was living happily ever after.

When Sojourner's job at the freedmen's hospital ended, she made plans to move back to Michigan with Sammy. Like many others, she was tired and disappointed. People thought the old woman had earned the right to go back home and end her days, sitting quietly in her front-porch rocking chair. They were wrong. When an editor asked her if he could write her life's story, she answered, "I am not ready to be writ up yet, for I still have lots to accomplish."

The Last Battle

Sammy, now a teenager, went everywhere Sojourner did. Her energetic grandson carried bags and helped her in and out of trains, remembering her cane when she dropped it. Sammy sold her books and photographs. He also read newspapers, signs, and books to her. When she needed to send letters, Sammy wrote them for her. He had become the wonderful son that poor scarred Peter could never be. Elderly Sojourner had finally healed from the terrible abuse she suffered as a child. She was ready at last to be a good mother.

Together they traveled throughout the country as Sojourner spoke for her causes. She often started her speeches by saying, "Children, I have come here tonight like the rest of you, to hear what I have got to say." As always the crowds were mostly white people. They listened as her strong voice called on them to provide land for freed blacks.

In the spring of 1870 she visited the new president, Ulysses S. Grant, to tell him what she had seen in her travels. She told him what had to be done to set things right. She liked his answers so much she told him she'd support him if he ran for president again.

He signed her autograph book, but over the next few months he made none of the changes Sojourner had suggested. Sojourner knew that he wasn't the only person who made laws. Congress did too.

One spring morning Sojourner and Sammy climbed the marble staircase of the Capitol. She gave a speech to a roomful of senators and representatives, pleading for land for the ex-slaves so they could begin new lives. "We have been a source of wealth to this republic," she told them. She said that after all the unpaid labor that black slaves had done, they deserved something in return.

Fourteen congressmen signed her book, but Senator Charles Sumner of Massachusetts did something much better. He promised that he would sponsor a bill in Congress based on her plans if she could prove that many citizens agreed with the idea. Sojourner knew she was right. She just needed to bring back proof of the truth that was out there.

Sojourner had Sammy write a letter that demanded "a portion of public land in the West" and "buildings thereon for the aged and infirm" for every freed slave. She and Sammy carried this petition with them everywhere, and thousands of people signed it.

"Lift up those people," she argued in churches, tents, fields, and town halls. "Teach them to read part-time and teach them to work the other part of the time. Do that, and they will soon be a people among you!" People who heard her took copies of the petition and got even more signatures.

A year later Sojourner stormed back to Washington ready to deliver the petition to Charles Sumner. The ex-slaves would be taken care of at last!

But Senator Sumner had just died.

Sojourner asked other senators to take on the project. No one wanted to help. Her year of difficult travel, the thousands of signatures, the hundreds of speeches—all were for nothing.

Her hopes crushed, her energy and health sapped by the traveling, Sojourner decided to go home to Battle Creek. She had to wait for Sammy, though. He was feeling sick—too sick to travel. Since he was only twenty-four, fit and strong, Sojourner thought her precious grandson would bounce right back to health. Instead he grew weaker. His cough got worse. His fever rose, and finally he died.

Sojourner had always expected to lose her slave children. She had known they could be sold away at any time. But not Sammy! He was her cherished "son"—the closest thing she ever had to a normal family. And now he was gone . . . young . . . strong . . . and gone. Sojourner wept a lifetime of tears.

Tired, old, and sorrowful, Sojourner did go back to Michigan. Her friends and family nursed her faithfully. Sojourner now lived in a little house on

Cottage Street. Her big old house was full of her children and their families.

Frances Titus, a friend who had helped Sojourner with revisions of her *Narrative* over the years, helped to rewrite it now with even more information. As she had before, Frances included newspaper articles about Sojourner, letters to her, and speeches she had given, along with the information from the first *Narrative*. These new editions were sold under the title *The Book of Life*. Frances began managing Sojourner's finances, too, and she read the mail to her and wrote letters for her old friend.

Gradually Sojourner's strength came back, along with her need to be active. Sammy was gone, but Sojourner's causes were not. "Life is a hard battle anyway," she told her friends, "and if we can laugh and sing a little as we fight the good fight of freedom, it makes it all go easier."

She tried to vote in the next presidential election. Again she was turned away, but not before she had made an angry speech to everyone who would listen. Women *should* be able to vote, just like men. And she wanted it to happen before she died.

Within a year she was traveling again. There was still more to do and her mind was strong, though her body was growing weaker. In place of Sammy her friend Frances traveled with her to Kansas, where a large number of ex-slaves were moving from the South.

Sojourner's main cause now was voting rights for women. She still spoke of land grants for slaves, argued for their education and demanded an end to the Jim Crow laws. But she had new causes now.

Slaves seldom had money of their own. Now that they were free, ex-slaves had money to spend. Sojourner was upset by how much they spent on alcohol. They couldn't keep jobs when they were drinking, and they couldn't raise healthy families. Sojourner, who had lived a long, energetic life after giving up alcohol, thought everyone should stop drinking, and she told them so.

Tobacco should be given up too. Sojourner knew that, firsthand. For the first time since she was a teenager, Sojourner wasn't smoking her pipe. She felt so much better that she wanted others to quit. Then she thought about how much money she had spent on sixty years of addiction and she got angry. If she only had that money now! She added a new cause to her speeches, pleading, "Stop your smoking!"

She also felt that the law was going too far when it sentenced criminals to death. She shook her finger at her audiences and scolded, "The person who wants to see his fellow beings hung by the neck until dead has a murderous spot in his heart!"

She spoke at women's rights conventions, and churches, and city halls, but her trips were shorter now. Eighty-year-old Sojourner's mind might be going strong, but her body was giving out. She was in great pain. For a long while she had suffered with ulcers on her legs, and now they were spreading. In 1883 she finally gave in and went home to Battle Creek.

She checked into a hospital run by Dr. John Harvey Kellog, a man she had known since she first moved to Harmonia. He had fresh, new ideas about health and medicine. He felt that what you ate was very important. He invented brand new health foods like corn flakes, and told people to eat them for breakfast with milk. His new-fangled treatments kept Sojourner more comfortable, but even she knew they could not save her life.

Her faith never failed. Her mind kept working too. Reporters still interviewed her. Friends came by, and she tried to be the old Sojourner for each of them. She told one of them, "I'm not going to die, honey; I'm going home like a shooting star."

In the dark of a starry night on November 26, 1883, eighty-six-year-old Sojourner slipped away without a word to anyone, her voice stilled at last.

Over a thousand people came to the Libyan Sibyl's funeral. Two minister friends, both white, spoke about her skill as a preacher of God and her good works. A parade of mourners, all dressed in black, followed her body to the cemetery in Battle Creek, where she was buried near her beloved Sammy. The whole country mourned her death.

Buildings, parks, and libraries were named for her so people would remember how she'd fought for equality. Postage stamps, souvenir T-shirts, and paintings have shown her face so we don't forget this powerful woman. Many books and plays have been written about her. The books she and her friends wrote are still in print.

Up in the sky, on a dark night, you see the same stars that gave lonely little Belle strength. Among them glows the dim red planet Mars. On the Fourth of July in 1997 a spaceship from Earth landed there. A small robot crawled out to take pictures to send back to NASA scientists, who then shared them with the world. That robot, a traveler through a strange new land, was named "Sojourner" after Sojourner Truth. It is still up there, shining on you every night, a monument to a woman who changed the world you live in with the power of her voice.

Progress has been made toward every one of Sojourner's goals, but there is much more left to do.

Thirty-seven years after Sojourner's death, the Ninteenth Amendment to the U.S. Constitution finally gave all female citizens of the United States the right to vote. Today half the votes in the country are cast by women. It takes a long time for a ship to change course, though, and women still get elected to only a tiny number of the spots in government. They do not have half of the total power. Women still make less money than men do for the same amount of work. And the country still does not have an Equal Rights Amendment.

Separate schools for blacks and whites were outlawed in 1954. President Lyndon Johnson signed the Civil Rights Act of 1964 and a Voting Rights Act the following year to make sure that everyone has equal rights under the law and that those rights are protected at voting places. But in some places blacks are still given a hard time at the election polls. And the Ku Klux Klan still meets to plan terrorist acts against blacks and other groups of people.

People are still arguing today about capital punishment, the use of alcohol and tobacco, and the repayment of blacks for the labor of their slave ancestors.

The country continues to improve. Changes are made by people who care enough to speak out about the things that matter. You can be a voice for change, just like Sojourner Truth.

For More Information

Today's Books

Adler, David A. *A Picturebook Of Sojourner Truth.*
   New York: Holiday House, 1994.
A clear, simple telling of Sojourner's life for younger readers. Lovely illustrations.

McKissack, Patricia, and Frederick McKissack. *Sojourner Truth, Ain't I a Woman?* New York: Scholastic, 1992.
For older grades, this book includes more detail about Sojourner's time and the people she knew.

Mabee, Carleton, and Susan Mabee Newhouse. *Sojourner Truth, Slave, Prophet, Legend.* New York: New York University Press, 1995.
A historian's in-depth perspective for adult readers.

Recent Editions of the Books Sojourner Truth Sold at Her Speeches

Gilbert, Olive, and Sojourner Truth. *The Narrative of Sojourner Truth*. Dover Books, 1997.
In this reprint, you can almost hear Sojourner herself dictating her memories to Olive back in 1850.

Truth, Sojourner. *The Book of Life: Sojourner Truth*. London: Black Classics, the X Press, 1999.
This is a reprint of the collection of writings Frances Titus put together in 1884.